# THE CRYPTO-CAPERS
# IN
# THE LEGEND
# OF THE
# GOLDEN
# MONKEY

## BOOK 3

Renée Hand

NORTH STAR PRESS OF ST. CLOUD, INC.
St. Cloud, Minnesota

To Ralph Wojtowicz, Jr.
Thank you for taking the time to help me. I couldn't have created such a wonderful tale without you.

Thank you also to Spencer Foerster and Emmanuel Watson for taking the time to create two of my new characters. You will read about them in the story. Their characters were of their own creation and I am thankful to them for allowing me to use them.

As always, thank you to my family for supporting me in this series, and by helping me with whatever I have needed. My heart is overflowed with appreciation and love.

Cover Art and title page by Alla Dubrovich
Text Illustrations by Corinne A. Dwyer

Copyright © 2009 Renée Hand

First Edition: September 2009

ISBN-10: 0-87839-330-7
ISBN-13: 978-0-87839-330-5

Printed in the United States of America.

Published by
**North Star Press of St. Cloud, Inc.**
**P.O. Box 451**
**St. Cloud, Minnesota 56302**
northstarpress.com

# A NOTE TO THE READERS

I hope everyone is enjoying the series. *The Legend of the Golden Monkey* will take you to Mexico, and though this is a fictional story, there is much to learn. The history of the places you will be visiting, as well as some information about the culture and beliefs of these great civilizations, are true. I learned a lot and I know that you will too.

In this case, you will be solving cryptograms, as usual, but remember that you will need to create your own cipher key.

Clues are given to you throughout the story so be prepared to take lots of notes. Make sure you also pay attention to the fine details of the story, just like the other books in the series. That's very important! There is much going on and much to remember. Each book in the series gets harder and more challenging. So, I hope you are feeling challenged. If you are having difficulty, create a sheet of two-letter and three-letter words. Star the most commonly used. This will definitely help you.

Some of the new things you will be learning about is how to use Mayan Math. Make sure you hang onto your notes from book three because you'll be using them to solve book four. Keep every book in the series because you'll have to refer back to them frequently and in the near future. Contest questions, teacher guides, and story activities can be found on my website for all books at www.reneeahand.com

The game is afoot, and the Crypto-Capers love a good mystery. Have fun solving the case along with the Crypto-Capers. Good Luck!

RWEODN FO EHT DWLOR

Renée Hand

P.S. Your first clues to help you fill in your cipher key.

K is for H, A is for L, and Y is for C.

# PRELUDE

"WHERE IS IT?" THE VOICE DEMANDED from inside of a shadowy hood. The old man, Dante De Luca, looked into that sinister face and knew he was staring at death itself. But death waited to claim its next soul. This specter wanted something else entirely. Giving up his soul might be easier. His aggressor was clothed entirely in black with a black cape draping over his skeletal shoulders like a curtain. The hood shadowed the face beyond identity, and all Dante knew of the man's build was that he was slender, bony almost, yet filled with unexpected strength. The man's grip on his wrist assured him of that.

And this terrifying visage was angry, furious. Even if Dante could not see the man's eyes, he could feel their glare. Having been awakened in the middle of the night, Dante was at a huge disadvantage. Standing in his torn green pajamas in his drafty vestibule, he felt as much embarrassed as terrified. His hair was tousled, and he could feel the stickiness on his lips of dried drool. His hand kept trying to hide the torn pocket and missing buttons of his comfortable old pajamas, and he curled his hairy toes, wishing he had remembered to put on his slippers. Clearly, had he known he would be confronted at his front door in the middle of the night, he would have prepared better. But, to the hooded man's question of where *it* was, the old man found himself unable to say anything. Instead of a response, his mind framed the hope that this was all a dream.

The old man's eyes flickered to the street, hoping someone passing by would save him from the intruder. But it was the middle of the night—no pedestrians, no traffic to speak of, certainly no timely patrol cars. The street was, in fact ominously quiet, and to add to the eeriness of the occasion, it had started to rain. Specks that shined like diamonds landed on the edge of the porch, catching the light from the hall. His cell phone lay on his bedside table upstairs, his wall phone was in the kitchen in the back of the house. Dante knew he had few options open to him. He could not escape this hooded spectre who had confronted him, and his old heart was thrumming loudly in his ears.

"I am losing patience old man," growled the hooded man. "Where is it?"

"What are you talking about," muttered Dante, his voice shaky. "Use a noun. Look, if you tell me exactly what it is that you want, perhaps I can help. But this is an intrusion. It's late and I'm tired. Come back tomorrow when I can think."

The hand on Dante's wrist tightened. In a hiss of supreme anger, the voice said, "I want the Mayan tablets. Two Mayan tablets were missing from one of the ruins."

Dante's mind raced. Fear climbed his throat. A confused look on his face was his only response.

The hooded man reached into his pocket, and Dante's mind nearly exploded with the idea that he was pulling out a knife to slice his throat or a gun to shoot him. Instead the man produced a drawing and held it close to Dante's face. Even with it right in front of him, it took a moment to realize he was supposed to look at the drawing the paper held.

"You know what I'm talking about. This. Look at this. Please do not feign ignorance. The marks on your cheek speak the truth."

Dante's other hand went up to his face. Two parallel lines trailed down his right cheek. Dante ran his fingers along his cheek, remembering how this had happened. His attention shifted back to the hooded man when he spoke.

"The tablets I speak of" said the man with ponderous precision, "were rectangular in shape, about the size of a brick, but thinner. One has the hieroglyph of a jaguar on it, while the other—an eagle. Years ago you stole them from one of the Mayan ruins." Contempt dripped from the man's voice.

The elderly man shook his head. There were some things in his past that he regretted. The stranger let go of his wrist and grabbed hold of Dante's pajamas and shook him instead. Dante heard that pocket tear a little more. He focused fearfully on the shadowy face, still unable to see its detail. He did see, however, that the man was waiting, waiting for an answer, and none too patiently. His wraithlike body vibrated with intensity.

3

Dante swallowed. "Yes, well . . . yes, when I was younger . . . there are things . . . some things that . . . I regret—"

The hooded man hissed like an angry cobra.

"Okay, I did that. I stole the Mayan tablets from one of the ruins in Chichen Itza, but . . . and I've regretted it ever since. Regretted that my whole life."

"Where . . . are . . . they?" the hooded man said, biting the words.

Again Dante swallowed. "I . . . I hid them. I did it . . . to keep the world safe." He paused briefly, gathering his courage. "You want the tablets because you think they'll open the chamber of gold, that the legend of the golden monkey is real, but . . . but it's not real. If you think it is, you're a bigger fool then I was. Yes, my brother and I opened the chamber decades ago, but there was nothing there. Nothing. There were no ancient artifacts, no gold—at least not there. In that chamber, you'll find only pain and disappointment."

"You *hid* the tablets?" spoke the stranger, ignoring Dante's explanation. "Where are they hidden? You tell me. I need to know."

Dante had awakened completely now and, for some reason, the bulk of the fear he had for this decidedly sinister-looking figure had left him. Now he was getting angry. "Didn't you hear what I said? There's no gold in the chamber. No gold. You won't find the item inside that I know you seek. The fifty-pound Golden Monkey is not there. Its worth would surely make all your life's

4

problems go away. I can empathize because when I was younger, I desired the same thing, so I will relay to you a secret I have learned. Forget what you came here for. Walk away. Let it go. There is nothing in that treasure room but desolate space, I promise you. Nothing. Nada. Zilch. Your quest is futile. I hid the tablets to prevent others from suffering the same fate that I have. Don't search for them, I beg you! They'll be your downfall."

The stranger grabbed Dante again by the front of his pajamas and shook him. This time, a good portion of the old fabric ripped away.

"I don't care about your warnings! They're the whinings of an old man. I'll ask one last time. Where are the tablets?"

Dante began to laugh to himself, realizing that the man in front of him was a fool. The answer was so obvious, but he didn't utter it. Only one other person alive knew the location of the tablets—of *one* of the tablets, and Dante trusted him with his life. The choice had been made decades before and not easily. But the tablets had been hidden and in different places. For a brief moment Dante's glance slid back inside his house, his eyes focusing on the painting of a weeping tree. Next to it sat a small wooden box. He then half smiled as he turned towards the stranger.

"All I have to say is this—are you an expert at solving puzzles?" The old man laughed out loud this time. "You better be."

The hooded man drew in a gasping breath as he felt a sharp pain. A bony hand reached up to his own neck, and he let the old man go and hastily looked around. Then he shoved the drawing back into his pocket. Again he reached to his neck and when he pulled back his hand, a smear of blood streaked across his fingertips. The hooded man closed his hand into a fist. His gaze shifted out the door, as if he were looking for something.

A little confused about what had happened, Dante caught movement in the hedges at the road, then heard the sound of footsteps running. The stranger turned quickly, but there was nothing to see. After a moment, Dante saw a silhouette across the road near a big maple tree. For just a moment, he thought it looked like the boy who had visited him earlier in the day. He had called for a computer tech to come and fix his computer. It was running slow and locking up often. He was certain he needed to update his software, but was skeptical about doing it himself, not wanting to cause himself more frustration. Dante had to admit that the boy impressed him. He not only fixed and updated his computer, making it run quicker and more efficiently, but he also helped him with his Internet connection and his cable TV. Dante had the urge to yell for help but swallowed the temptation as his eyes returned to the man in front of him.

Then, as abruptly as the stranger had come, pounding at his door in the middle of the night, he left, leaving the old man standing in the doorway in confusion, listening to the sound of his retreating steps and the slow rain. Dante saw the hooded man look up at the Tower of Pisa in the distance, grunt loudly in anger.

Then the moonless night swallowed him. Dante returned inside, closed and locked his door carefully and considered whether he should just stay up or go back to bed.

MORRIS WATCHED WITH SATISFACTION as old Dante closed his door. He didn't know who the old man's visitor had been, though he had an idea, but the discussion at the door hadn't looked very pleasant. And since the old man appeared helpless, he'd taken a few covert steps to help.

As Morris watched the hooded man leave, he wiped away the rain drops that had fallen onto his glasses. His clothes were starting to feel damp and heavy, but he was determined to ignore it. After all, Mr. De Luca needed him, and Morris found the man very interesting. He'd been an archaeologist in his youth, at times maybe even a treasure hunter, but he was currently retired. Morris had read about him in a *National Geographic Magazine* dated several years previous. He had been well known, but now only seemed to be a faded memory. Because of his exploits to Chichen Itza, Morris thought he might know about the lost treasure there, and the legend of the golden monkey. For years the legend of the golden monkey had been merely a myth, a story made up for entertainment, but in his gut Morris knew it was real. The conversation he had overheard confirmed his suspicions. When his father was told to go to Italy for a computer assignment, he had decided to take the family with him. Morris had no choice but to go, but being an expert in computers himself, he had offered his services to his father, and in so doing, allowed him to visit Mr. De Luca and help him with his computer problems, while hoping to get information from him.

While he had made some extra money vetting Mr. De Luca's electronics, Morris had also tried cajoling the man, trying to get him to open up, but he would have none of it. Mr. De Luca had never told him anything. Morris had been disappointed, of course, but now felt a little redemption with what he was seeing. Mr. De Luca didn't want to talk to anyone about his past, even when he was threatened. Whatever he was hiding, the pain of it still haunted him.

# ONE

MAX SAT BACK IN HIS SEAT feeling anxious. Turbulance caused the private plane to shake and jostle. With the artifacts they had found in Red Rock Canyon stowed in the hold, they were on their way to Mexico. Then, as quickly as the turbulance had started—it stopped. When Max turned, he saw Mia staring out the window, taking a break from the book she'd been reading. Granny was writing a letter, a smile on her face as she did so. The turbulence wasn't affecting her one bit.

"Are you writing Reggie?" Max inquired.

She met his eyes. "Yes, he asked me too."

"I know. I just didn't think you'd do it."

Her expression turned slightly amused. "Come, come, now, Max. It's not that big a deal. We . . . had a moment there when I was using him as a distraction for the crowd while you rifled the chest on the pirate set. I've talked to him on the cell phone a couple of times. He's nice."

"That restaurant he took you to was pretty posh. Must have money."

Now Granny rolled her eyes. "Money is far from everything. The dinner we had together before he left for

London was remarkable. He made me feel special. I haven't felt that way . . ." Granny's voice trailed off. She smiled, a little embarrassed, and returned to her letter writing.

Max, the consumate detective wanted to ease Granny's discomfort, "He reminds me a lot of Grand-dad."

Granny looked up, her eyes filled with affection. "He reminds me of Harold, too. He has the same color hair, the same mustache."

Max smiled. Granny rarely talked about her husband. He had been a detective, like the rest of them. Sherlock Holmes' blood had coursed his veins through and through, right down to his stubbornness. But he was no longer with them.

Max remembered the story vividly. Harold had been on a mission in Venice, working a mystery case, when he was attacked and pushed into a canal. Reportedly he had drowned, but the body was never found. The authorities had searched for days, but to no avail. Max's dad had been devastated, and frustrated with the Venice authorities for not being able to find his father's body. Granny had been upset as well, but she seemed to handle it better, at least in front of everyone, though Max remembered hearing her sob behind closed doors at night.

All that had happened five years ago and Max knew Granny missed her husband. Every once in a while he'd catch her reminiscing, knowing that she was thinking about him.

"Granny, why don't you just e-mail him? It'd be faster, you know."

Granny raised her head, a tranquil expression on her face. "You're probably correct, Maxwell, but then the letter wouldn't be as personal, now would it? If I hand write the letter, it shows that I actually took the time to express myself. It wasn't slap-dash. That, and I pride myself on having good penmanship."

Max glanced over at Granny's letter and realized that Granny wasn't writing her letter in English. Granny was fluent in various languages and dialects. In college, she had graduated with a language degree. Not only could Granny read and write various languages, but she could speak them fluently, with little to no hint of her English decent.

"Out of curiosity, Granny, will Reggie be able to *read* your letter?"

Granny smiled mischievously, then gave a little laugh. "If not, I guess he'll have a wonderful time trying to figure it out."

Max shook his head and focused again on the sheet of paper in front of him. He read the letter Maggie Devereaux had left for them once more. They were headed to the Riviera Maya, Mexico, a place of beauty and mystery, but they were not going there to relax. No, their stay was all business. Max remembered vividly the painting he had seen in the Panther's secret lair of the massive Kukulcan pyramid called the Castle, also known as "El Castillo." It is located near the center of Chichen Itza, which was strategically in the center of the Yucatan Peninsula, not far from the Riviera Maya. This bothered Max and filled his mind with unanswered questions, but it also intrigued him.

Max glanced at the pictures Maggie had included with the letter. They showed the ancient artifacts they had found. After staring at them, he could still not make a connection to what the Panther wanted from them. The artifacts were several large pieces of pottery, a Mayan plate decorated with a type of hunting scene, clay dishes and bowls, as well as some arrowheads and spears. If the pieces were sold, the value of just one could be ten thousand dollars, but Max could not believe that the Panther was after the money.

*Why go to all of this trouble?* If Max knew nothing else, it was that the Panther had some other goal in mind. *No, the Panther was after something else, but what?* Max then looked at the back of the picture of the the artifacts. He saw two letters on it. Before Max could continue with his thoughts, he heard the pilot's voice over the speakers notifying them of their descent. As he looked out, the billowy white of clouds around them soon opened up to a view of trees, water and earth.

They seemed to be coming in fast, yet Max couldn't see the airport. He heard the flaps come up and the wind rushing over them. The plane descended quickly, then banked in a rather sharp turn, and the private landing field came into view. The plane lined up on one ribbon of tarmac and dropped down to meet it. They landed smoothly. Max let out the breath he hadn't realized he was holding, then the roar of the engine being thrown into reverse filled his ears. The plane slowed. It taxied up to a shedlike building and stopped. They had arrived. Max quickly organized the pictures in his hands and tucked them into his pocket. When he looked up, he realized that Mia was talking to him.

"Ready to go?" She had her backpack slung over her shoulder, ready to debark.

Max rose and grabbed his backpack.

At the door they looked out as the hot tropical humidity washed over them, almost taking their breath away.

"It is so beautiful here," commented Granny as they descended the stairs, already beginning to fan herself.

They could see lush jungle and, just a short distance from the airstrip, some lovely homes sheltered among trees. Suddenly, a breeze kicked up and washed over them like a waterfall, giving them a brief reprieve from the heat. As their eyes gazed at the surrounding jungle, tree branches swayed to the rhythm of the wind, their leaves fluttering like graceful butterflies.

When they reached the ground, they noticed that men had begun to unload the boxed artifacts. These they took to an awaiting truck. The three Crypto-Capers spied a jeep waiting for them and walked toward it. Standing by the jeep was a handsome young man with tanned skin. His short ebony hair blew softly by the breeze, causing it to look tousled. His clothes were light in color and his smile emanated friendliness. As they approached, the man said, "Are you the Crypto-Capers?"

Max noticed that the man looked American, but when he shouted to the men unloading the plane it was almost in perfect Spanish.

"Yes, we are," said Granny. She extended her hand to him. "I'm Nellie Holmes, and these are my grandchildren, Max and Mia."

He shook each of their hands. "I'm Pablo. It is nice to meet all of you. I was thankful to hear that you were coming to help us with our situation. What's happened has left us very much confused."

"Oh? What's going on here?" asked Max. "We were not informed of the entire situation."

The handsome man smiled warmly. "Well, first let's get you settled into a hotel. The Rivera Maya is a tourist town, so you will find many wonderful and entertaining places here. Please, get in."

Pablo offered Granny an assisting hand, and she allowed him to help her into the jeep. Max and Mia climbed in, while Pablo loaded their bags into the back. Pablo then got in, waved to the pilot, who was still in the cockpit, and drove off. The truck followed behind for some time, then turned and went into another direction.

"Where is the truck going with the artifacts?" asked Granny.

"To a local warehouse until they can be identified, labeled and inspected. Then they'll be returned to the government."

The scenery around them was breathtaking—mountains, jungle, the flashes of brilliant birds and sounds of exotic animals. Around every corner they saw something new. In the open jeep, they also enjoyed the breeze that seemed to caress their cheeks and lift their hair. Max closed his eyes and reveled in the feel of it against the background heat of the jungle. When he opened his eyes, his gaze again took in the enormous trees on either side of the road. The thick canopy nearly blocked out the sunlight, making him feel as if they were in a tunnel. It was mysterious and a little intimidating, yet exciting.

"Is that airfield used often?" asked Max.

"Oh, yes," said Pablo, "this is one of a few private communities in the area, and has its own airfield. Many of the people who have homes here have their own planes. They come and go as they please without government interference. If you landed at the other local airfield, you would have been surrounded by police, taken into custody, and questioned relentlessly about how you came upon the artifacts. Stolen artifacts of any kind are taken very seriously down here. It is their heritage. Heavy fines are given, as well as jail time. By landing here, you are virtually undetected, especially when you were flying in my airplane." Max, Mia and Granny all glanced at each other.

"*Your* plane? But you weren't flying the airplane," stated Max.

"No, no! Of course not. A friend of mine, an

archaeologist, was your pilot today. You'll meet him later after he puts my plane back into the hanger."

"Pablo," started Mia. "Do you live in one of the houses along the airstrip?"

"Yes! We have passed it already or I would have shown you which one. It's handy living here, too. My permit to fly extends all over. I travel around Mexico and South America doing research. I am also an archeologist. The Mayan sites around here are amazing, as well as the Aztec ones, and I love the Incan sites in the Andes. I study all of them, which is why your team and I will be working very closely together."

"What association do you have with Maggie Devereaux?" asked Granny.

Pablo smiled, as if enjoying this inevitable question. "Maggie Devereaux is my cousin."

# TWO

"MAGGIE'S YOUR COUSIN?" Max said in surprise. Then he glanced at his sister and grandmother to see their expressions, also surprised.

"Yes. I am also aware that the Crypto-Capers numbers more than you three. Good day to you, Morris," said Pablo.

Morris's voice came disembodied from among them as if he were some kind of ghost. "Good day to you, Pablo. You didn't say you were Maggie's cousin when we spoke earlier."

"Well, in all fairness, Morris, you didn't ask."

"So, how many times have you two spoken?" asked Mia.

"Twice, once with Maggie, and then a few hours ago. I told Pablo when you would be arriving. Hello, team. I'm sure it's beautiful down there."

"It's beautiful indeed. I wish you would join us," commented Granny. "Won't you? You deserve a break after the last case."

"I would love too, but you know . . ." Then Morris started on with his litany of excuses and com-

17

plaints while everyone else mouthed his words in silence and rolled their eyes, mocking him.

"Yes, yes, we know," spouted Mia. "The humidity! The heat! Your asthma! The *insects!*"

"Exactly!" interjected Morris. Then he added, "Now, everybody wave, you're on Candid Camera." Pablo, Max, and Granny, raised their arms high and waved, while Mia stuck out her tongue. "I saw that Mia."

"I thought you had a hard time seeing the fine detail of people on satellite," said Mia.

"I did! In Las Vegas, I was having such a hard time keeping tabs on you guys. The signal kept breaking, even on the watch phones, but now . . . now everything's different. I have a new system to work with."

Max's forehead began to furrow, but then a smirk formed on his lips. "Is that what our dear Maggie was talking about?" Max was referring to Maggie's words when they were watching *The Orchid Menagerie* at the Mandalay Bay in Las Vegas the week before. She had said more than a few things that night that confused him, but the main comment he was thinking about was when she had said that Morris was in need of a few things. Max knew that updating their satellite link must have been one of them.

"Yes, it was. Now, no matter where you're at, I can see and hear you more clearly. After consulting with Maggie, she admitted on using a scrambler, but even without that, I was getting interference. It was the same when you were in Florida, so I knew it must have been the system. Remember what we talked about a few days ago?" Morris was referring to the conversation they had about fixing their weaknesses. The Panther had focused on their weaknesses in Las Vegas, trying to spin them into confusion, but the Crypto-Capers had been able to overcome his plans and succeed in solving the case.

"I remember clearly. We made an agreement," answered Mia.

"Yes, and I'm going to make sure that we're a solid team once more. We're to have more strengths than weaknesses," finished Morris.

Everyone in the jeep agreed, even Pablo.

It took over an hour to get to the hotel. For most of the trip, they were surrounded by tall jungle trees. Now they were on an older road, an ancient road actually, that seemed to cut between the trees perfectly, leading them to an unexpected place. Max closed his eyes, thinking of the history this road had seen, and wondered what they were going to see. When he opened his eyes he noticed that they passed a gate. Leading where, he was not sure. He had missed the sign. He waited with anticipation as they drove further, the scenery around them changing, opening up. The jeep stopped in front of a beautiful hotel. Its walls were white and clean, a good color in the sun-washed jungle and one that helped keep the interior of the hotel cooler. The building was surrounded by concrete flower beds filled with flowers in a made grouping of color and redolent of frangrances that beckoned them to sniff their perfume.

"This is the hotel where we will be staying. I reserved two rooms, one for you and one for me. It is better if we stick together. Feel free to get out and look around. I will only be a moment." Pablo walked into the hotel, leaving Mia, Max, and Granny to admiring the scenery and the gardens. The trio got out of the jeep and walked up steps that led into a beautifully landscaped area. The hotel exuded simple elegance.

Granny walked closer to one of the three pools, the bigger one having a small fountain in its center. She

wiped the sweat from her brow with a small white hanky. The sun in this tropical jungle beat down on them harshly compared to London or even sunny Florida and the desert country of Las Vegas. The water in the pool appeared clear and inviting.

Before Granny could step closer to the water, maybe run her fingers through its coolness, she suddenly glanced up, looking around at the nearby jungle that seemed to surround and weave into the hotel grounds. Her eyes caught sight of something moving. A cage full of monkeys.

As she watched them, Granny noticed some jungle monkeys working their way to the cages. After several loud calls back and forth between the caged and free monkeys, the wild monkeys reached into the cage with long arms and tried to steal the captive monkeys' food.

"You shouldn't be doing that," tutted Granny to the intruders, as she pointed her fingers at them, but they only screeched loudly at her. Granny raised her hand to her chest, saying, "Well, for goodness sakes, do what you want then, but don't shout at me. Really, how rude."

The monkeys called to each other, waving their arms, while others looked on in curiosity. Granny didn't think it was the first time these local monkeys had stolen food. They were much fatter than the captive monkeys, probably because they stole the caged monkeys' food, then returned to their tall trees and gathered more from the bounty of the jungle.

Pablo came out of the hotel, waving at them. "We are just over here. Let's take our things and go up."

The foursome returned to the jeep and grabbed their belongings, then followed Pablo back into the hotel and up a set of stairs to their rooms. They walked down an enclosed hallway lined with photos of the area. When they arrived at their room, Pablo opened the door and held it open so everyone could go in. Pablo then went to his room, which was right across the hallway from them.

The three London detectives progressed only a few steps into the room before the beauty of it stopped them. The room was immaculate. The walls were light and accented in mahogany. A fan slowly rotated above two beds covered with white comforters. Two wooden stands stood like servants at the end of each bed. To their right they glimpsed the bathroom and were impressed with the large footed tub and the tasteful decorations. Fresh flowers graced a nearby table to their left.

"Pretty," said Max with amazing understatement.

"Yup," Mia returned.

They laughed and set about stowing their luggage and gear. Granny went into the elegant bathroom to splash water on her face.

A few minutes later Pablo knocked on their door and asked to be allowed in. Max opened the door for him, and the four took seats in a nice grouping of chairs and sofas in front of a big window.

"You wanted to know what this is all about?" Pablo began. "I will tell you what I know. The artifacts that were found, as you already know, are Mayan. They originally came from Chichen Itza, stolen many years ago. Early archeologists—if I dare call them anything more than thieves—often took away priceless Mayan history. Over time, the artifacts were found and were then preserved in a museum. However, a few months ago, someone broke into some of those museums and stole the artifacts. Who, at the time, we did not know, but now we think it has something to do with this, this Panther fellow.

"Maggie said you are familiar with the Panther's movements. It is our hope that you can give us some insight to why he stole the artifacts." Pablo reached into his pocket and pulled out a piece of paper. "And why he left this."

Mia accepted the piece of paper. Before she opened it, Pablo said, "I believe it's a cryptogram." Sure enough, when the folds of the piece of paper were lifted, there was a cryptogram staring at them.

```
C  H    Z  Q    Q  A  Q  T  Q  X    C  B  E  C  A  Q  M  '

A  W  C  C  A  Q    G  X  R    M  A  H  D  .
```

"There is no key, no help whatsoever," said Mia as she began to work the cryptogram, the fact that she didn't have a key not bothering her one bit.

"No, wait a minute," said Max as he reached into his pocket for the photos of the artifacts Maggie had taken. He remembered the letters he had seen on the back of some of the artifacts. Max quickly perused the

THE LEGEND OF THE GOLDEN MONKEY

photos and then held up a few, showing everyone. "These artifacts have different letters on them. G is for A, Q is for E, and C is for T. See if those help, Mia."

Everyone watched as Mia plugged in the letters. She then used those letters to help her solve the cryptogram.

(This would be a good time to create and start to fill in your cipher to use as a key.)

| A | B | C | D | E | F | G | H | I | J | K | L | M | N | O | P | Q | R | S | T | U | V | W | X | Y | Z |
|---|---|---|---|---|---|---|---|---|---|---|---|---|---|---|---|---|---|---|---|---|---|---|---|---|---|
| G |   |   |   | Q |   |   |   |   |   |   |   |   |   |   |   |   |   |   | C |   |   |   |   |   |   |

"

_____

_____

_____

_____," read Mia.

"What is that supposed to mean?" asked Pablo. Max and Granny glanced at each other and shrugged. Mia raised her fingertips to tap on her lips as she analyzed what she had written.

She looked up, saw they were all watching her, and said, "Now, knowing the Panther like I do, I'd say that this message means nothing."

"It has to mean something," blurted Max, looking both confused and annoyed.

"Oh, it does, but not what we think. Let me try something." Mia took the beginning letters from each word and wrote them down.

———  ——  ———  ———  ———  ———  ——  ———

She then rearranged the letters several times until she got the result she was looking for.

———  ——  ———  ———  ———  ———  ——  ———

Max looked at what Mai had written and snorted loudly. "The beast is taunting us. He knew exactly what he was doing when he took those artifacts. He wanted to lead us here."

"Why?" asked Pablo, curious.

"Because, he needs us to help him find some things, and I guarantee he doesn't know where they're hiding," replied Max.

"What are we talking about?" asked Granny.

Max was about to answer, his mouth open and ready to retort, when Morris spoke instead. "The Panther's looking for the ancient Mayan tablets of Chichen Itza."

Pablo bolted to his feet, tripping on the edge of his chair, almost falling to the floor. Max stood quickly and caught him.

"Thank you," murmured Pablo, regaining his balance.

"What about those tablets bothers you, Pablo?" asked Granny, her keen eyes narrowing on Pablo.

The man, clearly still upset, said, "The Mayan tablets were stolen many years ago from Chichen Itza.

They are said to open a chamber of gold, a chamber supposedly holding an unimaginable amount of riches, but it's known for one in particular. Inside this chamber was said to rest a fifty- to sixty-pound golden monkey. As you know, with the price of gold today, that adds up to a lot of money." He caught his breath, ran a hand through his black hair and said more calmly, "You see, in the beginning of the nineteenth century, Europeans were coming to South America, visiting the many ruins. Some were explorers, some were amateur archeologists who wanted to know more about the great ruins, and some were thieves looking for anything worth stealing. These tablets were said to have been hidden in the walls of one of the ruins, where the Jaguar and the Eagle meet.

"There were supposed to be two small recesses, and inside those recesses were carvings of a jaguar and an eagle. That is the place where it is believed the Mayan tablets had been placed. I have studied these ruins, and have seen various carvings of jaguars and eagles. They are quite amazing."

"Do you believe this golden monkey exists?" asked Mia.

"I don't know. I've studied all the ruins, but have seen no evidence that the chamber exists, nor the infamous golden monkey, but would it be impossible? No! The one thing I've learned about being an archeologist is this: all ruins are full of mystery, and not all the mysteries have yet been discovered."

"Has lots of gold been found here?" asked Max.

"Gold has been found everywhere in the ruins of Chichen Itza. A metal as maleable as gold has always been in great abundance in the Mayan and Aztec ruins, and it has been found in many forms. I've seen gold pendants that represented Mayan rulers. Gold arrowheads have come from this region, as well as sacred cenotes. But the artifacts that have impressed me the most are the gold pectoral discs. Some were embossed, depicting certain events. The detail of these pieces can't be duplicated today, but they have all been preserved in museums. But not all treasure is made of gold."

"What do you mean?" asked Max.

"There is value in other artifacts, like the ones that you have returned to us. Mayan plates, pottery, lances—all are things important to the Mayan history."

"Can you take us to Chichen Itza?" asked Granny.

"Yes, of course. That is why you are here. I will show you!" Pablo smiled and stepped, not to the door, but towards the balcony. He swung wide the French doors and stepped out, breathing in the flower-scented air around him. He waited until Granny, Max, and Mia had joined him. What they saw amazed them. Thousands of trees formed a solid green wall, but within the seemingly impenetrable green jungle were gaps. From within those spaces rose tall stone structures.

"The ruins are this close to the hotel?" Mia exclaimed.

Pablo nodded. "We can go at any time, but first let us go down to the restaurant and have a good meal.

They have wonderful food here. My favorite is their grilled burgers—the meat is so tender and juicy."

Before he continued, Pablo turned around, and the team followed him from the room and out into the hallway, closing the door behind them. They walked down the staircase, and, once reaching the bottom, turned to the right and headed towards the restaurant, continuing with the conversation. "A portion of the food is grown on the property," Pablo explained. "The hotel sits on a hundred acres of beautifully landscaped gardens, some of which are vegetable plots. It's the largest of any hotel in the area, and it sits in the heart of Chichen Itza's archeological park."

# FOUR

PABLO WAS RIGHT, THEIR LUNCH was delicious. After eating, the foursome returned to their rooms to prepare for their excursion into Chichen Itza. The Crypto-Caper team unpacked some of their equipment and laid it out onto a nearby table. Max tested the laptop and the connections. Morris confirmed that everything was working properly. Then each person prepared a daypack, including the essentials they might need from their large equipment bag, including a bottle of bug spray.

Mia made sure she had her notepad, as well as extra pencils, and the fingerprint scanner. Max grabbed his Master Ring, which jangled as he set them inside of his backpack, his Leatherman, his magnifying glass, along with Cuetips, gloves, and double sided tape. While Granny packed two different kinds of cameras, one regular and another specifically made to use in the dark. She then handed Max and Mia some bottled water, some candy bars and granola for a snack, and flashlights that stored and used solar energy—no batteries.

Pablo walked in as the team was preparing and was amazed at their preciseness and automatic efficiency.

They were like a well oiled machine, each having a specific job and each doing it harmoniously without a lot of chatter and questions.

"Are you ready?" Pablo asked.

"Almost," said Granny as she slipped her arms into the straps of her backpack and adjusted the straps. Max and Mia did the same.

"Well, I have some choices for you. We can walk through Chichen Itza, but it will be getting dark in a few hours and we won't be able to explore much, and, believe me, when it gets dark here in the tropics—it's dark. Or, we can ride horses. There's a stable on the property. I feel that riding would be our best choice. We'll be able to get their quicker and, when it does get dark, arrive back here faster as well. Would that work for everyone?"

"We're all accomplished riders," said Granny, "so there'll be no problem there."

"Good! Shall we go then?"

As Pablo let the way down to the lobby, Max and Mia exchanged concerned glances. Granny muttered under her breath, "I just hope I get a horse that listens to me this time."

The memory of Granny being dragged by a foot in the stirrup made both Max and Mia wince. Granny knew how to ride and had done so numerous times, but some horses reacted badly to her. She wasn't cruel to them, by any means, but for some reason they just didn't like her. In London, Granny had taken them to their riding lessons. They had been riding through the woods and through various types of terrain, practicing their commands. It was their last lesson. When they were back at the stables, Granny had dismounted but one shoe had gotten caught in the stirrup. Before she could untangle herself, the horse had taken off and dragged her across the paddock by the time they were able to stop the animal. Granny had gotten away with sore muscles and hurt pride, to Max and Mia's relief.

"Let's keep an eye on her," whispered Mia, and Max nodded in agreement.

Four horses had been saddled for them, and were waiting as if the stable man had known of their plans. Granny was allowed to choose her horse first to aid in a good match. It seemed to be a quiet gray mare. Mia, Max, and Pablo chose from the ones left. Once mounted, Pablo took the lead and led them down a wooded path towards an open grassy area. The sun beat down on them harshly. The cool interior of their hotel room was soon forgotten as they began to sweat profusely. The humidity of the area filled their lungs, making it hard to breath. As they sat on their horses, their bodies struggling to adjust to the temperature, bugs began circling their heads. They all began to swat and jerk about.

The first place they wanted to go to was the Great Pyramid. The trip was scenic—views of tall trees filled with birds and small animals. Butterfies fluttered across their path, and insects called from high above. As they rode, they came upon several different parts of the ruins, and noticed how the jungle was reclaiming any area not recently and actively maintained.

The trail led almost to the center of the site. Their first stop was to an area known as the Observatory. Here they dismounted their horses, and tied the reins around the branches of some nearby trees before setting out on foot.

As they explored they noticed that the Mayans had had an intense interest in the sun traveling across the sky. Many of the ruins were set up to face the sunrise or sunset. They visited a ruin just south of the main temple known as the Carocal. Pablo played the guide for them as they went along.

"Do you see the windows of the Carocal? Several of them point towards the equinox sunset and the southern and northernmost points on the horizon where Venus rises. The Mayans were big in astronomy." He paused as they walked up the steps. "Some of the ruins have been reconstructed. Time has definitely done its damage but, amid all of that, you can still visit almost all of the ruins."

Pablo led the group to a portal in the massive stone structure. "Should we go inside?" asked Granny as she eyed the doorway skeptically.

"Absolutely! Exploring is the best part about coming to Chichen Itza, but keep in mind to be careful. We do not know what we are going to find. Nature has been slowly but surely reclaiming the ruins—both the encroaching jungle and the animals that live there. We do not want the wild beasties eating us for supper." Pablo smiled as he led the way to the opening. As they entered, the sun shone through gaps in the walls. The walkways were narrow. There was one room on their left draped in darkness. Bravely, they stepped inside. The space had a musty smell. Even after all this time, the smell remained from the past. The walls of the room could not be seen in the darkness, and an eerie feeling washed over them. Prickles crawled up Mia's spine.

"Good enough for me," spouted Granny as she rushed out of the room. Max and Mia began to laugh, until something brushed up against their legs nearly knocking them over. Their hearts raced. The intruder was silhouetted in the sunny opening—a meter-long iguana. They watched as it flailed its lizard way from the room, heading back to the forest. When Max and Mia looked around, they discovered that Pablo had also bolted from the room.

"Brave souls they are," commented Max with mock bravado, as he too, headed rather quickly for the portal opening. Mia, about to follow him, paused. Something seemed to call to her. She hastily removed her flashlight from her backpack and shined it on the wall. What she saw amazed her. Not only were there multiple layers of dirt and cobwebs on the wall, but an indention shaped like a large rectangle. Mia moved closer to analyze the space. When she was right in front of it, she raised her hand and touched the carvings. On one side of the rectangle was a jaguar, while on the other was an eagle. Pablo had been correct. Mia was standing in what must have been the treasure room.

Mia raised her arm slightly. "Max?"

"Yes, Mia? You coming?"

"I need you to come back, and bring everyone with you. I may have found the treasure room and the tablets."

# FIVE

BY THE TIME PABLO, MAX and Granny's voices could be heard echoing down the hallway, Mia had already removed a piece of paper from her backpack and was making a rubbing of the indention. She held the flashlight on her shoulder, locked in place by her cheek and shoulder.

"You've found the tablets?" asked Pablo as he moved by her side. Max hurried to Mia's side as well. He helped her out by taking the flashlight and shining it where she needed it. Granny was hanging back by the door letting her flashlight pan around the room.

"Thanks, Max! My neck was starting to hurt."

"No problem." Max then focused his next words on Pablo. "Are these the tablets you were talking about?"

Pablo raised his hand and touched the outline of it from Mia's rubbing.

"These are the indentions for the tablets. When we find them we must place them here."

"And that will open the treasure room?" asked Granny, not moving from her safe spot by the door.

Pablo turned his head towards Granny.

"Supposedly, but I'm not positive. It could also be nothing." When Mia was finished with her rubbing, she removed the paper. When she did, Pablo ran his fingers over the stone carvings. "These are amazing." He then ran his fingertips over the outline again, but this time he felt a slight indention near the center top. His forehead furrowed in confusion. "Either the tablets are curved slightly when they meet, or there's something else that needs to join them."

Max looked, and Pablo showed him the curve. He felt it, getting an idea of the shape this other object would have to be. Mia moved closer to the door to check if the rubbings were detailed enough. As she stared at the picture she noticed something. To the center of the tablets, sitting in between the jaguar and the eagle, was a circle. In the middle of the circle was an image of the main temple of Chichen Itza, and above it the sun seemed to be angry as it watched over it. Two birds were flying above the temple. "Granny, could you take a picture of that?"

"Sure, dear. Max, train your light on the spot," replied Granny as she removed her camera from her backpack. She adjusted the lens. Getting as close to the wall as she could and have the area in question in the shot, Granny took several pictures. She also took a picture of Mia's rubbing. When she was finished, Mia rolled up her paper, paperclipped each end so it wouldn't unfurl and tucked it into her backpack. Then Granny put away the one camera and took out her other one and started to get ready to use it.

"Are you sure the camera works in this low light?" Pablo asked.

Granny smiled. "Well, I wanted a couple of shots with the flashlight just in case, but this camera has a special infrared lens that allows us to take pictures in the dark. But there must be complete darkness. If there's any light at all it'll be blinding white, nothing else." Granny stepped forward, told the boys to move out of the way for a moment and had them block the entrance as much as they could. She took several pictures. She then covered the lens and returned the camera to her backpack.

"When did we get that?" asked Mia. "Was it in the box that Morris sent?"

"No, I picked it up in Las Vegas. It's amazing what you can find there." Then Granny directed her next words to Morris. "Morris dear, did the images come through clearly?"

"I'm getting them now. I'll analyze the pictures and tell you more in a few minutes. That new camera worked great, though. From the look of it, those pictures are clearer than the other camera's."

Granny smiled with pride.

"I must say, it was one of my better purchases, though I wasn't sure if I connected what I needed to properly for you to receive the pictures. I was concerned about that."

"You did fine, Granny. You're more technologically savvy than you think," complimented Morris with a disembodied chuckle.

Mia, her flashlight back on her shoulder, made notes of what they had seen so far. Max had gone back to the indentation and was feeling it carefully. Something interested him. He felt some bumps and some scratches. "What's this?" he asked Pablo.

Pablo leaned close and saw the bumps and lines. "Those are . . . numbers."

Max looked at them again. "Numbers?"

"They're Mayan numbers. They had a base-twenty system. Each number was represented by a symbol. Now, if I remember right, each raised dot represents the number one, and each scratch or bar represents five." Pablo looked around and saw Mia's notepad. "Can I use your notepad for a minute?"

Mia handed Pablo her notepad and pencil. "Here you go." She and Granny trained their lights on the site for a larger brighter image.

"Thanks, Mia. Now, here is an example of what I'm talking about." Pablo started drawing dots and bars.

"A dot means one. The bar means five. So, if I drew something like this . . ."

"It would be the number eight. With me so far?" Pablo glanced, seeing that they clearly had followed this. "Now, if you did a sequence like this you will see that we can turn these numbers into a math problem." Pablo continued to write the numbers down. "The top number is multiplied by twenty, while the bottom number is multiplied by one."

●● $= 2 \times 20 = 40$

●●● $= 3 \times 1 = 3$

"When added together we get forty-three. Make sense?"

Everyone nodded.

"Good, now let's look at the indention again." Pablo trained Mia's flashlight on the bumps and scratches and noted them down on Mia's notepad. This is what he saw.

(Write down the numbers you get on the lines.)

"Now, because the dot and bar groups are not on top of one another, we are not going to add them together. We're going to keep them as is.

_____ and _____."

"So, what do these number mean to us?" asked Granny.

Pablo sighed. "They could mean anything. These bars and dots were not made by the Mayans, though they're like what the Mayans used. These appear to be scratched in by someone else, someone . . . more recent. I can tell you this was done many years ago, probably decades, not centuries. To know actually when they were created isn't possible. My guess would be that they were created to remind the person who stole the tablets where they were hidden—maybe?"

"You're reaching pretty far there," stated Max.

"Well, it's my only guess, but it seems logical, doesn't it?"

Suddenly, Morris's voice came over Mia's watch phone. "Mia, the picture you rubbed resembles some type of sundial that the Mayans had used. I don't know much more than that. From what it looks like, this sundial was the centerpiece of the tablets, joining them together. So we are now looking for three pieces—not two. Personally, why a sundial would be down in a dark hole of a room, is beyond me, but I'm just the computer expert. What do I know." Morris paused for a moment, and they could hear the tapping of his fingers moving rapidly over the keyboard.

"By the way, you have a group of tourists coming your way, and I think our discussion has been over heard. There's a fat man that looks like a flower garden sitting outside the main portal ahead of the group. It appears that he might be resting, but one can never be too careful. Wait—he's on the move to join his group."

"Should we question him?" asked Mia as she glanced towards Granny.

Before Granny could answer, Morris piped in, "He's wrote something down on a piece of paper and shoved it into his pocket. It may be nothing, but what I know from experience is that we need to keep an eye on the flower garden—I mean we need to keep an eye on the fat man. Sorry, but from up here the man looks like a mound of pink flowers, especially when he stands still."

The Crypto-Capers and Pablo quickly stowed their gear in their backpacks and returned to the main portal of the ruins. They saw the fat man talking with members of his group several feet away. He looked like a tourist, camera and all. They returned to their horses. Their next destination—the Great Pyramid.

# SIX

WHEN THEY ARRIVED AT THE GREAT PYRAMID, they were amazed at what they saw. It was huge and impressive. Erosion had eaten away parts of the stone steps but that did not take away from the beauty of it.

"Can you imagine what it would be like living back in the time of the Mayans? These ruins are amazing," said Max as they dismounted again.

"We've picked a good time to come. The park is closed to outside visitors. Only those who are staying at one of the hotels inside of the park can come here. Fortunately, because of the time of day, there are not very many people about. That group behind us will be the last one for today. Come, I want to show you something special. It'll take some time, but I want to climb the steps. There's something very interesting you'll want to see at the top before the sun sets."

"Absolutely!" replied Granny.

"Good, now please follow me, but be careful. The steps aren't in the greatest of shape." As everyone moved to the edge of the pyramid and looked directly up at the massive structure, Pablo said, "What's unique about this temple is that when standing at the foot, you could shout loudly, but what you hear in return is a loud shriek. But, if you're on top of the temple and speak in a normal voice, anyone below can hear you."

"How does that work?" said Mia.

Pablo shrugged.

They began to climb the ancient stairs, except for Granny. Max was the first to notice. He stopped and turned around, trying to balance himself on the steep, narrow steps. "Aren't you coming?"

Granny placed her fists on her hips and raised her eyebrows, her whole manner shouting loudly, "Are you kidding?" but instead of saying the words that Max knew she was on the verge of speaking, she said sweetly, "I think that I'll watch over the horses. You go ahead without me, dear." Max nodded his head and smiled, as he turned around and continued up the stairs. He'd thought her enthusiam sounded a bit forced.

The climb was strenuous. Max and Mia stopped half way to catch their breaths. Pablo stopped as well, his hands on his hips while his chest rose and fell quickly. The trio glanced down at Granny, who was starting to appear smaller, and waved at her. Then they continued up the stairs again. The sun was getting lower in the sky.

"Hurry, I don't want you to miss this," spoke Pablo, moving faster up the stairs.

When they finally reached the top, panting and wheezing for breath and drenched in sweat, they were rewarded with an amazing sight. All the ruins could be seen, and they were laid out almost in a line. Pablo waved Max and Mia over to him. "Here, this is what I wanted you to see."

They joined him as the sun fell toward the horizon and dusk. As they looked down the steps they had just come up, they saw a serpent form down the tall pyramid.

"Oh my . . ." started Mia.

"Giddy aunt," finished Max. The scene before them was magical.

"The Mayan's built El Castillo to do this at dusk. It is an amazing feat."

As Max glanced at the serpent again in pure admiration, he followed the length of it all the way to where Granny had been standing. When he didn't immediately see her, his gaze flew to the left and to the right searching for her. The temple was in an open space, trees surrounded it but they were further out. There was no where Granny could have gone that they wouldn't be able to see her, and yet . . .

"Morris, where's Granny?" asked Max. Mia heard her brother and immediately began to walk around the top of the pyramid to see if she could see her. A tall stone cover over the center of the pyramid blocked her view, but other than that, the area was pretty open. Regardless of where one could walk, they could see everything below them. Mia could see a few people climbing down from the pyramid. One person in particular caught her attention. She couldn't tell if the person was tall or short, but knew that it was male. He seemed almost in a hurry, and he kept constantly glancing back. He was near the bottom of the stairs now. She then saw another person coming out of the trees towards him.

"How's the view?" returned Morris nonchalantly.

"I feel very small." Max said.

Morris laughed. "Granny is to your right, Max. You should be able to see her. Mia is glancing at her now. You might wish to move with haste though because it looks like she is beating up on some man."

"What's she doing?" Max's voice was filled with disbelief as he heard his sister say, "Found her! She's over here, hurry!"

Max and Pablo both rushed over to Mia's side. Max wanted to shout at Granny, but then he remembered what Pablo had said about their voices carrying from the top of the pyramid to the bottom, and raised his voice slightly to make sure he was heard. "Granny, what on earth are you doing?"

Before she answered, the trio saw her give the man a hard karate kick to the mid-section. "Oohh!" escaped Max's lips as all three cringed from the sight below them. The man fell to the ground, landing on his back.

Pablo recovered before Max and Mia did. As he glanced at the stranger longer, he realized that he recognized the man on the ground. He quickly shouted, "Wait, Granny, wait!"

Granny stopped her approach on the man and glanced around her as if she heard voices but didn't know where they came from. She looked like a ninja on the attack. Her knees were bent and her arms and hands were raised in front of her. But then she looked up and saw Max waving at her from the top of the pyramid. Then she heard Pablo say, "Please leave him be. He is a friend!" Then he waved to reinforce his words.

Max, Mia, and Pablo quickly began their descent down the stairs. Once she heard Pablo's plea, she relaxed her pose. In those moments, Granny changed back into a seemingly helpless old woman with a sweet and kind demeanor. Granny was a contradiction of many sorts, but that was her greatest camouflage. No one ever knew what to expect from her.

"I am so sorry, dear," started Granny as she moved closer to the man still lying on his back on the ground. "Here, let me help you up. I feel terrible." Granny reached out her hand to the man, a sweet smile on her lips.

The man was hesitant to take Granny's offering, not wanting to be thrown to the ground again. But after several minutes of pain trying to get up himself, he extended his hand to Granny. She pulled him up with ease. Her grip, belying her apprearance, was filled with strength.

The man muttered, "Thanks!" as he massaged his back, his other hand on his stomach.

"I do apologize again for the misunderstanding, but you did sneak up on me. I felt that my life might be in danger. A woman of my years . . ."

The man stared at Granny in disbelief but did not argue with her. He kept his frustration to himself. The pair stood side by side in silence as they watched Pablo, Max, and Mia, make their way towards them.

As Max focused on every step below him, not wanting to trip and fall to what would be a horrible death, he gazed upon the Nunnery—another Mayan building—briefly. It was a part of a southern group of ruins, a place believed to be the living quarters of the elite Mayans. Soon the building was lost again amongst the trees. The descent seemed much faster than the climb. When the trio's feet touched the ground in safety, each took several minutes to regain their breaths. Pablo was the first to speak.

"Granny, this is my archeologist friend I was telling you about. His name is Walter Regent."

"And I was also your pilot," Walter chimed in tersely. But Granny shrugged as if the information meant little to her. To be honest, she hadn't paid much attention to what their pilot had looked like. Her thoughts had been too consumed with writing Reggie at the time.

"What are you doing out here?" Pablo asked Walter. "I thought I suggested to meet us at the hotel?"

"I arrived shortly after you left for the ruins. I was hoping to catch up with you, but I wasn't sure where you were going, so I just took a guess. I was wrong on my first attempt, starting with the Temple of the Jaguar. When I finally made it over here, you were almost to the top. I went to ask this lady a question because she appeared to be waiting for you, but before I could get a word out, she attacked me." Walter glanced at Granny and then smirked as if he were a child telling on their sibling to get them into trouble.

"Attack is such a strong word," Granny said sweetly, playing up the old lady role. "From this point on let's just say that I strongly bumped into you."

Walter, looking incredulous, said, "Well, lady, you strongly bumped into my chest and stomach thus causing me great discomfort," retorted Walter angrily.

"Please do not refer to me as, 'lady'. If you wish to talk about me, call me Nellie. I in turn will call you Walter. And, Walter, I do believe you're taking this much too personally. I didn't mean to harm you. I was only protecting myself. A man of your youth can understand the perceived difference in our capabilities, can't you? What would you do if a stranger walked up to you and tapped you on the shoulder unannounced?" asked Granny.

Walter thought for a moment. "I can see your point . . . Nellie. I assumed that you'd seen me approach, but obviously you hadn't. I tapped you on the shoulder to get your attention, which was apparently elsewhere. But could you at least admit that you overreacted just a tad?"

Granny thought for a moment, then conceded. "Yes, fine, Walter, I'll admit I did overreact perhaps just a bit. Again, I'm sorry."

Walter smiled and nodded his head. "Thank you, Nellie. I'm also sorry for my temper. I don't want us to get off on the wrong foot. We'll be seeing each other quite a bit, and I really don't want tension between us."

Granny agreed and smiled. Then she took a good look at Walter. He was tall, with slightly long brunette hair and brown eyes. His skin was fair, though tanned, a contradiction to the time he must spend in the sun. She gathered that he must wear a hat. She noticed that his clothes were nice—a white shirt with tan shorts.

"Good," said Pablo, "now that all of that is settled, I think we should return to the hotel. In a few minutes we won't be able to see each other."

The group agreed. Before mounting, Granny, Max and Mia, removed their flashlights from their backpacks to shine ahead of their horses. When everyone was set, they headed back to the hotel.

# SEVEN

BY THE TIME THE GROUP ARRIVED at the hotel, it was pitch dark. As soon as the sun went down, the jungle seemed to swallow the light, and night animals created an eerie background music of calls and rustling. The occasional solar-charged light along the path marked turns and made their journey uneventful. After the horses were returned to the stable, the group made their way back to the hotel looking for some supper and a quiet evening. But as they neared the lobby, they heard music being played. The place was alive with people and entertainment. The pools were littered with guests swimming and laughing. The dining room crowded with people.

As they headed for the entrance they skirted the pools. Max noticed a boy about eleven years old watching them. His hair was short and dark with a slight spike in front. His face was tanned and he had a similar complexion to Pablo's. If Max was to guess—and he was always guessing about everything—he would say that the boy was from Venezuela. His apparel was casual—ripped jeans and a plain orange shirt—a statement of his youth. Max smiled as he walked by.

The boy watched each member of the group with interest. He smiled and nodded at Max, then at Granny, Walter, and Mia. His gaze lingered longest on Mia. With her long braids hanging down the side of her face, and her features, pure and sweet, he thought her very pretty. Then the boy's gaze fell upon Pablo, who appeared tired from his climb up El Castillo. His gaze was focused in front of him until he heard his name being called.

"Pablo!"

Pablo spun around before he saw the boy. Then his features illuminated, his eyes filling with excitement. "Spencer?"

The boy all but flew into Pablo's arms. Max, Mia, and Granny stopped and watched as Pablo hugged the boy. Walter had continued walking. It took him a moment to realize that everyone else had stopped. When he did, he came back to the pool, saw Pablo and the boy and said, "Hello, Spencer."

"Nice to see you again, Walter," spoke Spencer as he removed his arms from around Pablo's waist.

Pablo said, "Spencer, these are the Crypto-Capers, the detectives Maggie sent to help us. This is Granny, Max, and Mia Holmes." Pablo then placed his hands on Spencer's shoulders. "This is my brother, Spencer."

Spencer glanced at each person standing in front of him, smiled and nodded. "It is very nice to meet you all," he said. His gaze fell upon Mia and lingered a little bit, then Spencer's cheeks turned slightly pink.

"He's staying with me until our parents take him to the United States. They're going to be visiting Maggie, Lucille, and Juliet in Las Vegas for a week or so."

"You'll enjoy Las Vegas. There's a ton of things to do there," said Mia. "You'll especially enjoy the shows your cousins are in. Lucille and Juliet are talented. We had a chance to see them perform."

Spencer nodded and smiled. "I'm looking forward to that." Then Spencer added, as he turned slightly towards Pablo. "Have you eaten yet?"

"No, but I think we're all about ready?" Pablo glanced at the group and saw their nods. "Shall we head towards the restaurant then?" Walter led the way to the restaurant. The hostess seated them right away at a large corner table, and they ordered beverages and food.

While they waited, Walter began to tell stories about the Incas, the Aztecs, and the Mayans. He obviously knew much about those cultures and how they were unique and special.

"What I find interesting is that each group was similar and yet different," said Max. "They all worshipped a type of sun god. They were all builders of enormous cities and roads, rulers of vast empires, and yet were also contributors to science."

"Yes, but despite their wisdom, they were all eventually conquered by the Spanish, and because of that, much of their history was destroyed," added Mia.

"You're correct, Mia," said Spencer. "But, though the city of Chichen Itza of the Mayans and the city of

Tenochtitlan of the Aztecs were both conquered and pillaged, did you know that the Spanish didn't touch Machu Picchu?"

Mia, Max and Granny all focused their attentions on Spencer. "I thought . . ." began Mia.

Spencer smiled. "Oh, the Spanish did conquer the Incan empire, and they did so by using the Inca's own bridges made out of plants and vines as thick as my legs. These bridges were strong and had lasted hundreds of years. They allowed people to cross over dangerous rivers and to go from village to village in the mountainous terrain. If the Inca's would have cut those bridges down, the Spanish may have been defeated. But they didn't, and, instead, it was the Incas who lost." Spencer paused for a moment.

"But Machu Picchu is hidden in clouds about eight thousand feet above sea level. The Spanish never found it. Because of that, many of the artifacts there were still intact for archeologists to find. Some of these artifacts have given great insight into much of the Inca's life and astronomy."

Pablo and Walter both knew this bit of information, but Mia, Max, and Granny were impressed. They knew a little bit about the Aztec, Mayan, and Incan civilizations, but they didn't know as much as their companions. They absorbed the information like sponges. Then the food arrived, interrupting their history lesson. With everyone's hunger controlling them, the group ate quickly and with little discussion.

RENÉE HAND

When the meal was over, Pablo wanted to relate some Mayan legends, but Walter excused himself from the table. "The day's excursions have tired me, and we don't know what tomorrow will bring. See everyone in the morning." Walter laid some money on the table for his meal. The group said their farewells to him for the evening, and he left.

Max had been watching Walter's movements with interest for several minutes. He had seemed distracted by something. For a while he had listened to Spencer's discussion, but he glanced at his watch a little too often, as if he were late for something. Then, just before he left, he had yawned widely a few times. As the man left the restaurant, Max watched as he headed into the hotel. He didn't know why Walter's behavior had sparked his curiosity, but he thought perhaps he should keep an eye on the man. Then his attention focused again on the story Pablo was telling.

"My favorite Mayan legend is about the two greatest princes of all time. They were brothers who had tremendous strength and skill, but they were also very different in nature. The younger brother, Kinich, was kind and merciful. He was loved by all. But the older brother, Tizic, was sullen, his strength coming from hate and anger nursed in his heart. As the story goes, they both fell in love with the beautiful Nicte-Ha, and despite her many protests, the brothers declared a battle to the death for her favors. Their battle was longer and more hideous than anything the world had ever seen, until the brothers died in each other's arms. In the afterlife, they begged the gods for forgiveness and for a chance to return to the world of the living to see Nicte-Ha again. Their request was granted. Tizic was reborn as the *chechen* tree, which seeps black poison from its branches and burns anyone who comes near. While Kinich was reborn as the *chacah*, whose soothing nectar neutralizes the chechen venom. They solemnly watched over Nicte-Ha, who had died of grief, and was mercifully restored to life as a beautiful white flower."

"Why is this legend your favorite?" asked Mia. "It seems kinda sad."

"The legend talks of the battle between good and evil, greed and selflessness, love and hate. Women have been fought over . . . probably since there have been men and women. Unfortunately, in these battles for love, there is hardly ever a winner. Only after they were dead did the brothers realize how foolish they had been fighting over a woman, and yet neither brother lost his devotion for Nicte-Ha. Their devotion was admirable and yet foolish, wanting someone another has."

"One brother could have given in," Pablo pointed out, "wanting the other to be happy, but that wasn't what happened. The brother's fight destroyed the woman they loved, but they were too consumed by their own anger to see what they were doing to her. Nicte-Ha could not live with herself for causing such discord. She fell into despair over what had happened, but unfortunately, she hadn't been allowed to choose."

"Which one do you think she loved?" asked Mia curiously.

Pablo shook his head and shrugged. "The legend never says, but I think she loved them both. That was why she gave up on living. I think she was torn between them."

"That was deep, Pablo," spouted Mia smiling.

"Men can be deep," Pablo said. "We have a heart and soul, do we not? Am I right, Max? Spencer?"

"Yes, but most girls would not believe it," added Spencer quietly. Max agreed loudly in the background.

Pablo said, "Most women wouldn't either, but we spend our lives trying to persuade them that we do think beyond the moment. Sometimes our efforts are in vain and we seem shallow. In truth, we care about a lot of things. We are just not as free with our emotions as women are. For example, you would not see a man crying for no reason."

Mia rolled her eyes. Pablo cocked his head to the side and gave her a sarcastic grin.

"Pablo was just saying that girls are a little bit— weepy," commented Spencer.

"And boys are a bunch of whiners," spouted Mia, her annoyance showing.

Granny's eyebrows lifted. "Tut, tut, children, we'll have none of this." That ended the discussion, but Granny couldn't help but to add in her own two cents. "My husband, god rest his soul, was a man of heart and depth. He truly loved without reserve, always thinking of others before himself. Men have feelings. On the other hand, my husband was also half off his rocker and drove me crazy constantly."

Mia couldn't help but to stifle a laugh. Then Granny yawned and stood. "I believe that I shall retire as well. It's late, and as Walter said, we don't know what tomorrow will bring. Should we meet for breakfast in the morning before we discuss our plans for the day?"

Pablo smiled. "Sounds good to me, Nellie. Our adventures today turned up much to think about. I hope tomorrow brings clarity to it all."

Granny, Max, and Mia, said their good-nights and left for their room. Once there, Granny and Mia got ready for bed while Max sat in front of the computer talking to Morris, who had been listening the entire time to the dinner conversation.

"The legend of the two brothers was interesting," started Morris, "I checked into Pablo's family tree, and he does have a brother named Spencer. It seems Pablo's family's moved around quite a bit. They're world travelers of sorts, so I'd believe Spencer probably knows about the Incas."

Max took in the information, confirming what he already knew.

"What about Walter? Anything come up on him?"

"Bits and pieces only. He is an archeologist and has graduated from one of the top schools in the country. He's also traveled all over the world. He's worked with Pablo for a year now, and often flies his plane from one place to another doing research. I have a feeling that you have certain reservations about him. Correct?"

"I'm not sure," answered Max. "For someone who was such in a hurry to find us, was also pretty eager to go elsewhere tonight after dinner. It makes me wonder why. Can you track his whereabouts for me?"

"Only if you tag him," said Morris. "Put a tracking device somewhere on him, and I can monitor where he goes." Max thought for a moment and glanced at Mia, who was now climbing into bed. "We'll work on that. Thanks. I'll keep you posted."

"Good night!" Morris said before the web camera turned off. Max thought about what Morris had said before he too got ready for bed.

# EIGHT

EARLY THE NEXT MORNING, Mia and Max were the first up. Max mentioned his idea of tagging Walter with a tracking device. Mia had her negative opinion about doing that, but she knew that any kind of information that could shed light on what was going on would be helpful. So, she put a few tracking devices into her pocket. The device was a thin, clear piece of plastic, and would only activate once it was attached to an object.

The siblings left a note for Granny before finding their way down to the main floor. The morning sun streamed into the lobby, looking glorious. Max smiled and closed his eyes. When he again looked around, he saw that Mia was looking into the window of the gift shop. He joined her.

As Mia stared into the window of the shop at all the wonderful souveneirs, she noticed a boy standing behind the counter. In front of him was a large man with an almost bald head whose face was round and plump, and his neck shook as he moved. His eyes were small, almost piglike, his full cheeks pushing up against them. He was wearing white shorts that were too tight with a flowered shirt that made him look like . . . a flower garden. He slammed something down on the countertop, causing the boy to jump slightly in surprise and nod his head rapidly. The man started yelling loud enough to be heard in the lobby. "I need this translated and sent, boy. Where's your father? This is urgent!"

"He's sick, sir. He won't be in for a few days. I'm well versed in several languages. Italian is one of them."

"Can you do it?" the man hastily asked.

The boy glanced at the message. "Of course, sir. All I need is to know the number to where you want the message sent, and I will take care of it," replied the boy smoothly. "Or is it the same as the ones you gave my father?"

The man narrowed his eyes at the boy, then reached his chubby hand into his pocket and removed a number, slamming it down on the countertop. As the boy reached his hand out to take it, the fat man grabbed his wrist, pulling him halfway over the counter.

"It's different this time. This is to be kept private. Absolutely private! Say a word to anyone, and I'll make sure it's your last. Destroy the message after it's sent like your father did the others."

The boy nodded emphatically. The man removed his grip from the boy and reached his hand into his pocket again, but this time pulling out some money, which he slid over to the boy. The boy took it without question and reassured the man that the message would be sent and destroyed. The fat man glared hard at the boy one more time, then left.

Seeing the man coming their way, Mia almost felt as if she should hide. Feeling foolish for even thinking of it, she merely grabbed Max's arm, pulling him down the hallway to the entrance, saying she wanted to see the sunrise.

When the fat man left the gift shop, he walked in their direction. And when they paused at the doors, he inconsiderately bumped into them, basically shoving them out of his way and against the wall. Mia held up her hand protectively, touching the fat man's back as he passed, trying to keep him from squishing her. The fat man didn't say a word as he pulled up the waist band of his shorts around his rotund form and kept walking. His body moved side to side as he walked, his thighs rubbing together so rapidly that he could have started a fire.

Max and Mia glared at the man in disgust, not because he was obese, but because he had no consideration for anybody else, and it showed in his every movement.

After the man had disappeared, Mia and Max returned to the gift shop window. The boy was still alone, reading the message the fat man had given him. He laid the paper down and reached for something around his neck. It appeared to be a necklace of some sort. He lifted a medallion that had been hiding inside of his shirt, and glanced at it, ran his thumb across it before holding it to his chest. He then removed it from around his neck and placed it onto the countertop.

From somewhere behind the counter, a phone rang. The boy turned, opened a door and stepped inside another room to answer it.

Mia grabbed Max, and they went into the shop. All around them different types of reproduced artifacts as well as photographs and framed paintings of Chichen Itza were displayed for sale. Of course there were shirts and trinkets hanging everywhere as well. Mia, however, made a beeline for the counter. Her curiosity had been piqued. Max kept watch behind them as Mia hastily perused the countertop, though it seemed as if her attention was focused entirely on a basket filled with various medallions made of a type of gray stone. In the center was a circle that had a picture of a sun and the main temple of El Castillo carved into it. Something in Spanish was written on the bottom, but Mia could not make it out.

## S MARAVILLA DELMUNDO.

Two birds were also in the scene flying down towards the temple. The edges were carved in the Mayan style similar to the ruins. She then glanced at the one the boy had worn around his neck and was laying on top of the counter. It  was similar in shape and size to the ones in the basket, except that his appeared much older. Mia thought the boy's medallion was maybe an original, and he kept it close to his body because of its importance.

Mia reached into the basket and pulled a similar one out and laid it next to the one on the counter. The copy was much thinner, though everything else appeared to be the same. "Max, I have seen this before."

Before Max could reply, the boy came out and hastily covered the medallion with his hand. He slipped the necklace over his head and tucked the medallion into his shirt. "What can I help you with?" the boy asked softly as he took the sheet of paper the fat man had given him and put it below the counter, his eyes roving between Max and Mia. The boy was neatly dressed, tan shorts and a light-blue shirt. He had dark hair that was slightly long and fair skin. His eyes were a pretty chocolate brown that at times appeared soft and kind. The boy definitely didn't appear as one of the natives. His name tag read Emmanuel.

"Yes . . . well . . ." Mia stammered. "I was admiring this medallion. It is very unusual."

"It is not a medallion. This," the boy said as he pointed towards the basket, "is a sundial. Something like this was used many years ago by the Mayans. There are no originals left; they were all destroyed by the Spanish. These are nice copies of the ones Mayans may have used. I frequently wear one to show the customers. They are on sale," the boy finished as he folded his hands on top of the countertop.

Mia glanced at Max and then reached in her pocket, pulling out some money. "Then I'll take two." Mia dipped her hand into the basket and grabbed another sundial to join the one on the counter. As she did she knocked something from the counter. It landed at the boy's feet.

"I'm so sorry," said Mia as she leaned slightly over the counter to see what she had done.

"It was just a pen. No harm done." Emmanuel bent over to pick up the pen. When he did, Mia noticed a long scar across one of his kneecaps. It was an old scar, and as Mia assessed the boy's age as being close to her own, she knew it probably had come from a childhood accident. When Emmanuel rose, he glanced at Mia and smiled as he rang her up. Mia already had the full amount ready. Emmanuel put the sundials into the bag, as well as the receipt and handed it to Mia.

"I hope you are enjoying your stay at our hotel."

"We are. It's so beautiful here. We've been learning a lot about the history of Chichen Itza," replied Max.

"Well, there's a lot to learn. Are you here on vacation?"

"Not really," started Mia. "We're here helping a friend look for something."

Emmanuel's features turned serious.

"You are not treasure hunters, are you?"

Mia raised her hand to her chest. "Goodness, no. You can think of us more as . . . treasure protectors." Mia leaned closer to the counter. "What we find we give back to their rightful owners. We keep nothing for ourselves, and we are definitely not interested in stealing. We want to preserve history, not pillage it, and we are certainly not greedy."

Emmanuel smiled.

"My name is Mia, and this is my brother, Max. We're a part of a detective team known as the Crypto-Capers."

Emmanuel gave a soft scoff. "*You* are detectives?" He began to laugh. "*Junior* detectives perhaps?"

"As a matter of fact," said Max, his tone just a bit haughty, "we've moved beyond that title some time ago to the official one." Max removed his wallet from his pocket and opened it, showing Emmanuel his badge.

Emmanuel's expression clouded. "Is that real?"

"Of course it's real. I've worked very hard to achieve this level." Max caressed his badge with his thumb, then returned it to his pocket.

"I didn't mean to offend, or doubt. I've just never met detectives before . . . at least not ones so near my own age." Emmanuel paused and shook his head, then smiled before saying, "It makes me proud. Our abilities are so often doubted because of our age. I know how that feels. So, again, forgive me if I insulted you."

"Not a problem," answered Mia as she gave her brother a sideways glance.

Emmanuel looked at them with genuine interest now. "So, you're here because of your case?"

"Yes."

Emmanuel ran his fingertips over the sundial through his shirt. The gesture seemed protective.

"Well, then I'll let you get back to it. Thank you

so much for your purchase, and have a great day."

"You, too, Emmanuel, and thank you." Mia held up her purchase. Then Max grabbed her by the elbow and steered her out the door in a hurry. When they were in the hallway, Mia turned on her brother. "Why were you rushing me out of there?"

Just then Walter had walked up to them.

"Oh," Mia whispered.

"Good morning you two," said Walter. "I see we're getting an early start?" Walter's features appeared haggard, as if he had not slept.

"We were just getting gifts for friends back home. Souvenirs!"

Walter smiled half-heartedly and nodded. "Well, Pablo and Spencer are already in the dining area. I also just saw Nellie. She was looking for you two. She said that she was going to join Pablo and Spencer for breakfast, and if I saw you to tell you to join them."

"Thank you," said Mia. "We'll head there straight away." She turned, and her bag slipped from her fingers. Walter stooped to pick it up at the same time Mia did. Her hand brushed his shoulder. He handed the bag back to her with a smile. Then he continued on his way.

"Oh," said Mia, "which direction is the dining area from here?"

Walter pointed to their right.

"Thanks! We'll see you later."

Max and Mia headed for the dining area, while

Walter entered the gift shop. When they had put a little distance between them, Max brought his watch close to his lips and whispered to Morris. "Morris, the target is lit. Start tracking when ready."

A few seconds passed when Morris answered, "You mean targets, don't you?"

"What? No, Mia only tagged . . ." When Max glanced at his sister, the expression on her face gave her away. He grinned. "You put a tracking device on the fat man too?"

"When he bumped against us, it was the perfect opportunity. Besides, I have a feeling that we should keep track of him."

Max shook his head, though he knew Mia was right. Sometimes she just had a way of knowing things.

Morris said, "It doesn't matter to me who you tag as long as I can label them, so I'm not confused. Who's the target standing by the pools?"

Mia looked out towards the pool area. "The fat man," she said.

"Then Walter is currently in the hotel gift shop, correct?"

Max and Mia smiled as they glanced towards the gift shop. "You are correct."

"Signals are hot."

"As long as the tags remain in place, I'll be able to track their movements and tell you where they are. I'll keep you posted."

"Thanks, Morris." Max debated for several seconds, then decided to see exactly what Walter was doing in the gift shop and peeked through the window again just in time to see Emmanuel pulling out something and showing it to Walter. Walter removed a piece of paper from his pocket and wrote something down, which took him several minutes, then placed the paper back into his pocket. He patted Emmanuel on the shoulder and straightened up.

Max and Mia scampered to the dining area before Walter exited the shop and caught them spying on him.

"Max, I have seen that sundial before," Mia said. "When we were in the dark room at Carocal where I found the tablet carvings, remember how Morris said that the image between the tablets was a sundial?"

"Yes, I remember vividly."

"Well, what I just bought was a duplicate of that image. It's not the original of course, but we'll at least be able to compare the rubbing with the sundial and see if it's close in size. If it is, it might come in handy. If not, I believe we know where to find the original." Mia turned her head to glance at her brother, hoping that he'd noticed the same thing that she had.

"You are referring to the sundial that Emmanuel was wearing around his neck, aren't you?"

"Good, so you noticed the differences too?" asked Mia.

"You mean, did I notice the different thickness of the sundials for sale and Emmanuel's? Yes, I did, and I also noticed how Emmanuel was protective of it. But what caught my attention the most was the fact that he almost cherished it. Someone had given that pendant to him to protect, someone close to him, I'd bet."

"How did you get that information?" Mia asked with a snort. Max always seemed to pick up on the smallest detail.

"It was the way Emmanuel was holding it, Mia. Also the way he had tried to quickly remove it from our sight when he had caught us looking at the basket full of sundials. His behavior depicts the truth. He is a keeper of something, and we need to find out what."

They reached the hostess at the dining room.

"What do you think Walter was writing down?"

Max shook his head in response. He, himself, was puzzled with what Walter was doing. "I don't know, but what I do know is that Emmanuel is keeping himself busy helping everyone out. I think he's some type of informant. The fat man and Walter are going to him to send or to retrieve information. The question we need answered is, who is he sending information to and where is he getting his information from?"

Before any more could be said, the hostess directed them to where Pablo, Spencer, and Granny were sitting.

# NINE

"THERE THEY ARE!" SAID PABLO, and he smiled. Spencer had also smiled in greeting.

"And where have you two been?" asked Granny as Max and Mia sat down. Her voice was somewhat stern, though her eyes belied her tone.

"We were in the gift shop doing some shopping. Mia found some unique items to buy." Max's tone was casual, and he picked up a menu and stared at it intently.

Granny knew that something important had happened, but she let it go, figuring her grandson would fill her in later. Mia picked up her menu as well and perused the contents. When the waitress came, everyone at the table ordered. There was polite conversation concerning the schedule for the day for twenty minutes after that, then the table grew silent. Max took advantage of that opportunity.

"Pablo, what do you know about the boy in the gift shop?"

Pablo's forehead furrowed. "What boy in the gift shop?"

"He works there. His name is Emmanuel."

"I don't usually go into the gift shop, so I really don't know," replied Pablo.

"I do!" Spencer said. Everyone's gaze was focused on him now. "Emmanuel Watson. I've gone into the gift shop many times. I know Emmanuel pretty well. He's very nice, but likes to be mysterious. He's actually the grandson of an archeologist and wants to be an archeologist some day. He's actually quite knowledgeable about many things. He knows more about the ruins than any of us do, I can tell you that."

"That's interesting," commented Max.

"Is his grandfather still alive?" asked Granny.

"I believe so. Emmanuel hasn't made me believe otherwise," answered Spencer.

"Who is his grandfather?" asked Mia.

"I don't know, but I do know that he lives in Italy somewhere. He taught Emmanuel Italian, and he speaks it fluently. I've heard him on several occasions."

This new revelation caused Mia's eyes to widen. She cut a glance to her brother and nudged him with her knee. Emmanuel had been sending messages from the fat man in Italian. Could it be to his grandfather in Italy? Was he somehow involved in all of this? The news almost caused Max to stand up and approach Emmanuel about it right away. What stopped him was the knowledge that being rash was never a good option. He must strategically plan what he was to do if he wanted to get maximum results.

70

"Spencer, would you be interested in helping Mia and me with a little theory?"

"Sure, whatever I can do to help." Spencer's face lit up with excitement.

"What's going on?" asked Pablo.

Granny interjected, "Actually, that doesn't matter. What I'm interested in, is what you want Pablo and me to do?"

"We need you and Pablo to go back to the ruins today," said Max. "Look at some of the places we haven't visited. Spend some time there and take pictures, write random stuff down. Mia, Spencer, and I are going to stay behind. We have to find out what's going on with Emmanuel. He's funneling information for many people, including Walter and the fat man we saw yesterday at Caracol, and that man is sending information to someone in Italy." Max paused for a moment. "How is your Italian, Granny?"

"*Molto buono.*"

"What?"

"I said very good. I brush up on all my languages from time to time, Maxwell."

"Well, it helps when you have a photographic memory. I'll admit that I am envious of that quality."

"Don't be. We all have qualities that make us special. But it'd be beneficial if you learned a new language."

"I don't have the patience or the time. My mind is filled with too many things as it is. Besides, that's why we have you." Max smiled at Granny's disapproving smirk.

"How many languages do you speak?" asked Spencer, curious.

"I fluently speak English—obviously—but also French, Spanish, and Italian. I dabble in a few other languages," replied Granny. "But speak nothing else fluently."

"Wow!" Spencer was impressed. "I only know Spanish and English."

While the conversation was going on, Pablo couldn't help but to be worried about his friend. "Are you sure that Walter is involved in this, Max? He may have been just helping us gather information?"

Max could sense Pablo's devotion to his friend and he knew not to say too much too soon about Walter's possible betrayal. Not until he knew more. "I don't know what Walter's involvement in this is yet. That's why we need to find out. So, here is the plan." Max filled in everyone at the table about his plan. By the time he was finished, their food arrived. Everyone ate in silence, pondering what was to be done. When they were finished and left the table, they decided to walk down the hallway that Max and Mia had used an hour ago now. That was where Walter had found them, wanting to know what the plans were for the day.

Granny explained. "We're splitting up. You'll go with Pablo and me. We'll search the far side of the ruins, while Spencer, Mia, and Max, search the other side. We'll meet somewhere in the middle and see what we find. We must be thorough and cover every inch of Chichen Itza."

Walter reluctantly agreed with Granny. "But the children by themselves in a place like this, Nellie? Chichen Itza is a vast area full of potential danger. Are you sure they wouldn't be better off with an adult with them? Don't get me wrong, these are amazing kids, but they are children none the less."

"Children are swift. They'll be able to cover more area, getting into the smaller crevices of the ruins, putting them together makes more sense. So, you'll be joining me and Pablo."

Walter was about to comment but Granny's determined features showed no chance of her changing her mind. She was resolute.

"Very well!" Walter conceded. "But I was just thinking of the children's safety."

"That's sweet, Walter," began Mia. "But where do you think Granny learned her karate from?" Mia pressed her hands together in front of her chest and bowed.

Walter's eyes filled with disbelief, but when he glanced at Granny, she smiled and nodded briefly.

"Well, then my concern is unnecessary," Walter said. "Should we be off then?"

The group returned to their rooms to get what they needed for the day's journey. Max made sure he swapped some items from his and Mia's backpack into Granny's. While that was going on, Mia took out the sundials that she had bought from the gift shop and laid them on the bed. She took several pictures of the front and of the back of the sundials with Granny's camera.

"Morris, are the pictures coming through?" Mia inquired, then waited for a response.

"I'm getting them now. Give me a second, and I'll measure and compare the pictures of the tablets with your picture of the sundials."

"Let me know when you have something," said Mia before turning towards Max and Granny. "How are we doing?"

"We're almost set," answered Max.

Mia picked up the sundials and returned them to the bag. She was about to put them away when Granny asked to see them. Mia gave her one.

"I really think this does match the circle in the tablets that we took pictures of yesterday."

"I know. I think the original sundial is supposed to secure the tablets together in some way. I don't know how yet," said Mia. "I'm hoping a copy might work."

Granny ran her thumb over the front of the sundial, her eyes scanning the words below the picture.

"Maravilla Delmundo!" Granny thought for only a moment, then said, "Wonder of the world. This place is a wonder indeed. You might be right about the sundial. Can I see the other one?" Before Mia could show it to Granny, someone knocked on their door. Granny quickly gave Mia back the sundial and told her to hide it. Mia hid it where they hid all of their valuables, in a secret compartment inside of their luggage only accessed by a secret code. Granny motioned for Max to check the door. He saw Spencer, Walter, and Pablo outside.

"It's our friends," spoke Max quietly.

"Finish filling your backpacks before we open the door. I don't want them in here."

"Yes, Granny." Max called through the door, "We'll be right out." Then he hurried to help Mia with their backpacks. Morris's voice joined them as they worked. "The measurements are the same in the pictures and rubbing, Mia. From my calculations, the sundials you have do match the circle in the center of the tablets in the wall at Caracol. You're correct in thinking that the sundial holds the tablets together. Now, we have to find those tablets."

"Thanks, Morris," replied Mia.

"By the way, the tracking devices are working perfectly on Walter and the fat man, though you could have placed the device better on the fat man. His keeps jostling about."

"I was lucky to get it attached that well because I was squished up against the wall like a sardine. I placed it where I could."

"I was just saying, that's all," answered Morris, though Mia heard the underlying tone in his voice. It made her feel unappreciative.

"I know, Morris, and you do a great job. Next time I'll try and put the device in a better location. I'll work around the problem and think quicker on my feet."

"Thank you," replied Morris happily.

When Max, Mia and Granny were finally ready, they opened the door. Pablo was the first to greet them.

"Ready?" he asked, clearly eager to get started.

"Yes," said Granny. "Sorry for the delay. We were just trying to figure out what shoes to wear."

Pablo laughed, knowing that Granny had said this for the benefit of Walter and Spencer, who had rolled their eyes at the comment. Pablo knew exactly what was taking them so long to get ready, especially after already seeing how the team prepared for a day's excursion.

"I arranged for horses again to take us back into the ruins."

Granny nodded, and everyone headed to the stables.

# TEN

AFTER GRANNY'S GROUP LEFT, Max waited ten minutes before doubling back with Mia and Spencer towards the hotel. "So, what's the plan?" asked Mia as she tried to keep up with her brother's stride.

"Spencer, we'll need you to distract Emmanuel somehow to give us time to do a little snooping. We need to see what's back in that office behind the counter. Mia, you'll be helping me of course."

By the time the trio reached the gift shop, they noticed that the door was closed and locked.

"Now that's strange," commented Spencer. "The gift shop is usually open all afternoon and into the evening hours." The three of them looked through the window. The lights were turned off, but nothing seemed out of place. It really just looked like Emmanuel had closed up early.

"Where do you think he could have gone?" asked Mia, but her question went unanswered.

Max had gone to the door and taken something from his pocket. When he started fiddling with the lock, Mia knew he was trying to pick it. "Spencer, why don't we keep look out while Max finishes what he's doing."

Mia and Spencer moved in opposite directions from the gift shop door, one looking down one hallway while the other stared down the other. Spencer glanced at Mia, but when she looked at him, his attention focused somewhere else, almost embarrassed that she had caught him staring at her.

"You know, Mia," Spencer began, but couldn't finish.

Mia, not quite sure what was wrong with him, felt that she should say something. "Spencer, I'm sorry for yesterday. I think I was rude to you when we were discussing the meaning of the tale of the two brothers. I'm sorry if what I said made you angry." Mia paused for a moment as she studied Spencer's reaction. He looked flabbergasted. "I'm just—sorry!"

Spencer was moved by Mia's apology. Her words were the same ones he'd wanted to use but couldn't say. The fact that the Crypto-Capers wanted his help at all was something that he'd never forget. It meant a lot to him. He didn't want tension between him and Mia, and he'd felt terrible when he'd realized that he had angered her.

"Mia," he said, gathering courage. "I'm sorry too. I shouldn't have made my comment about girls. In all honesty, I feel that you're strong and smart. Personally, I don't think you're weepy, and my comment wasn't directed at you, anyway. It was just my observation about some girls in general." Spencer wasn't sure if what he was saying was making the situation worse or better, so he shook his head in frustration as he cast his gaze toward the ground. "Mia, I'm just—sorry! I'm sorry!"

Mia smiled. When Spencer noticed she was smiling, he smiled. "Thanks!"

Before anything more could be said, Max whispered, "Got it!" Mia rushed to her brother's side.

Max said, "Spencer, stay in the hallway just in case Emmanuel comes back. If he does, distract him. Make sure you keep him away from the door so we can get out when we're done."

"Here," Mia said as she removed her watch phone from her wrist. "Put this on. If you look to the side you will see buttons. One has a "G" on it—that's Granny. The other has an "M" on it, for Max. Press that one if Emmanuel is coming and warn us so we can hurry up. Okay?"

Mia did not mention that Morris could hear everyone's conversation at all times if he wanted to. She thought that bit of information should be kept to themselves. Especially when Morris channeled his reply to whoever's phone he wants. Their system, at times, was complicated. The technology of it, impressed them all, but as long as Morris knew how to contact everyone, that was all she and Max cared about.

Since Las Vegas, Morris had made some modifications to their watch phones to make them more accurate and fool proof. Now their signals could not be jammed as they had been in Las Vegas. That was the first problem that Morris wanted to rectify. He hated not being able to communicate with his team, especially in an emergency situation. That was when the technology he depended on needed to work the best.

"Any questions?" asked Mia.

"No, I got it." Spencer slipped on the watch.

Mia and Max entered the gift shop and closed the door quietly behind them. Once inside, they could see a light coming from the room behind the counter. The door was closed, but light still shone around the edges of the door.

"Morris," Max whispered into his watch phone, "are you able to detect untagged people?"

"Yes, when they're in close proximity to the watches. Why?"

"Because, there's a room ahead. I want to know if someone is in it before we open the door and get caught by them," whispered Max.

"Walk up to the door and turn the face of your watch towards it. Now, there is a tiny button on the edge of the back side of your watch towards the right. Do you feel it?" Max did as Morris told him to do and felt the button. He also noticed several more.

"I feel several buttons. What are they for?"

"In time, my impatient friend. My advice to you is this, though. Don't trim your thumb nail too short or you won't be able to activate any of the buttons. Just an FYI for you."

Max and Mia glanced briefly at each other before focusing again on their task.

"Now, when you're ready, hit the button."

Max pressed it and out shot a red beam of light. It began toward the left side and slowly worked its way to the right. The red beam suddenly shut off while Max and Mia waited for a result. It took several seconds to compute.

"The room is clear, Max. There's no one inside, but there seems to be some interference coming from the back of the room. Another door, perhaps. It's hard to tell."

"Thanks, Morris. We'll let you know soon."

Max took a deep breath before opening the door gently. When he had a big enough gap to peer through, he poked his head inside. Morris had been right, the room was empty. He then opened the door wider and stepped into the room. Mia quietly followed behind.

The room was neat and orderly, except for some pieces of paper scattered on the desk. These were the ones Max wanted to focus his attention on. As he glanced at the first piece of paper, he saw several mixed up groups of letters. The message was coded.

"This one is a cryptogram," said Max as he handed it to Mia. He then glanced at another piece of paper. He saw another cryptogram, then another. On each piece of paper was another cryptogram. "Mia, there are five cryptograms here, and two letters written in Italian."

"Well, we'll need Granny to translate, unless . . ."

"Don't even think about it," Morris broke in. "It'd take me hours to translate the letters. More time than I

81

have right now when I'm keeping track of so many things for all of you."

"Granny it is then," said Mia as she glanced at the papers Max was handing her. When she glanced up she noticed a pad of paper with the top sheet ripped off. "I see that someone's been working on them." With the papers still clutched in her hands, she leaned forward and studied the pad. It was strange how there were no indentions from a pen or pencil left on it. Next to the pad of paper was a piece of cardboard. That would explain it. Emmanuel must have placed the cardboard under the paper when he wrote. Clever! Clever!

She then noticed a drawing. Mia picked it up and stared at it. It looked like different levels of a maze. "Should we take all this?" asked Mia as she clutched the papers and the picture to her chest. "We don't know what's important and what isn't."

"No, we can't take anything. Emmanuel would know he'd been compromised. We want him to think that everything's as it was." Max paused for a moment. "Get out your little camera."

Mia felt her pockets and then quickly searched her backpack. The camera was the size a large nail file and was easy to hide. But she didn't have it.

"No, I forgot. I gave it to Granny so she'd be able to sneak pictures of things if she had to in front of Walter."

Max gave his sister a disapproving glare. Then his eyes searched around the room and noticed a copier in the corner. "Well, fine. We'll make copies of everything. Then we can work out the cryptograms away from here." He quickly began to make their copies.

The machine was loud as it heated up. The only benefit to it was that it was fast once Max hit the copy button. Mia kept glancing into the gift shop. When Max was finished he placed the papers back onto the desk in the same places he'd found them, as if he'd memorized where they'd been, which Mia knew he had. When they were about to leave the room Max noticed something on the floor behind the counter. The bucket in which the sundials had been kept in was on the floor. The contents were everywhere, but the sundials didn't look like they had just spilled. They looked as if they'd been searched through.

Max's eyes widened as a revelation hit him.

"We didn't do that did we?" asked Mia as she moved forward to pick up the mess. Max reached out his hand and grabbed Mia's arm to stop her.

"No, but I think I know who did and why." Mia stared at her brother in confusion.

Suddenly, Spencer's voice came over the watch. "He's coming! Be ready to get out."

Max, his hand still on Mia's arm, swung her into the room, closing the door behind them.

Max raised his arm slightly to whisper, "Morris, where's the interference you found earlier?"

"Oh," said Morris. "Go to the right of the copy machine."

Max and Mia hurried toward the wall Morris had specified and began to analyze it. The wall was made of wood paneling. Thinking of the hidden caverns they had found in Red Rock Canyon, Mia instantly ran her hands up and down the length of the wall. It felt like it had taken her a long time, but only a few seconds had passed when she felt a draft.

"Morris, how much time do we have?"

"I would say only a few more seconds. Spencer's doing a great job distracting Emmanuel—I can hear him—but Emmanuel seems to be in quite a hurry. His tone is clipped, sounding impatient."

"I feel a draft," Mia said, and she moved her hands up the wall to find the pressure point. She could not find an edge, the wall just kept going up. Mia stepped back, her brain working quickly on what to do.

Max was also studying the wall. Suddenly, he turned around and went behind the desk. Max quickly ran his fingers underneath the front edge. To his delight, he felt a button. With a sly grin, Max pressed it. The door to the secret passageway opened immediately.

"Let's take out our flashlights. We don't know what we'll encounter." Mia and Max both removed their flashlights from their backpacks and turned them on. Mia glanced at her brother, nodding to show she was ready, then moved hastily into the awaiting tunnel. Max quickly followed behind his sister, after he pressed the button to close the door, that is. It slid behind them, connecting with a resounding, "THUD!" that echoed down the tunnel, reverberating off the cold stone walls. Max shook his head and clenched his teeth, hoping they hadn't just given themselves away.

"Let's move!" encouraged Max as he pushed his sister forward. With the evidence held tightly in Mia's grasp, Max and Mia hurried down the dark, foreboding tunnel.

# ELEVEN

GRANNY, PABLO, AND WALTER HAD spent the past few hours searching the many different places of the ruins. When they had arrived in the middle of the grouping of Mayan buildings, Pablo and Walter thought they should wait for Max's group. However, knowing that Max was not going to be arriving, Granny diverted the group's attention elsewhere, feigning curiosity. She had taken several pictures here and there but it wasn't until they reached the Nunnery, which sat in the southern group of ruins, that they found something.

As they glanced around them at the amazing structures, Granny realized how well preserved they were. Pablo confirmed this when he said, "This area of the ruins contains some of the best preserved structures at Chichen Itza. The ruins in front of us are said to be the living quarters of the elite Mayans." The trio noticed that every square foot of wall had reliefs and paintings decorating them. The sight was impressive to behold.

As they looked around Granny noticed a recess in the side of one of the structures. Always the curious one, she led the way to it without thinking. She came upon a

large staircase. Towards the top was an ominous black opening. Smiling, Granny started to climb.

"Nellie, it might not be a good idea to go up there," warned Walter.

"I'm sure this recess has been explored by hundreds of others."

Pablo and Walter followed her up the staircase. Once she arrived at the opening, Granny took out her flashlight. She then gave the men a sly grin and entered the unknown.

With every step into the tunnel, the walls appeared to be slowly but surely narrowing in front of them. They had to stop and turn at several intersections before continuing. Suddenly, their journey ended at a dead end, a large piece of limestone blocking their way.

Not having explored the recess before, Walter stepped towards the wall and touched it. The limestone was hard and cold underneath his fingers. Suddenly, something long and furry moved over his hand. Walter shouted and bolted for the exit, knocking Granny and Pablo against the wall in the process.

"Are you all right, Nellie?" asked Pablo as he gazed at the space where Walter had been, his voice still echoing off the walls and his running footsteps fading.

"I'm fine, thank you, dear." In the melee, Granny had dropped her flashlight. When she stooped to pick it up, her foot brushed something, causing it to move. With flashlight now in hand, Granny focused its beam at the object. It was almost the size of a shoe box with different layers rising and lowering on top. Granny couldn't resist picking it up. When she did, the object felt fragile and old, even if, at the same time, it felt like it was made of stone.

Pablo had his light trained on her, but he was edging backwards, creeped out by the place. "Take it and go, Nellie."

Granny agreed and let Pablo lead the way. When they made it to the opening of the recess at the top of the stairs, Walter was nowhere to be seen.

"Where do you think he went?" asked Granny as she tucked the object she had found safely into her backpack to observe later.

"I don't know, but we better find him."

Granny agreed as she and Pablo started down the stairs to search for him. After fifteen minutes of searching with no result, Granny was losing patience. "Morris?" she called softly.

"Yes, Granny?" came Morris's pleasant voice.

"Could you be so kind as to tell us where Walter is?"

"Of course. Just give me one second."

Pablo turned to Granny. "How can Morris possibly find him? He can't know where he is all of the time." Granny glanced at Pablo and gave him a crooked grin.

"You underestimate Morris's abilities greatly. You'd be surprised what he can do. He's very resourceful." Granny, of course, didn't mention the fact that Mia had planted a tracking device on Walter.

Within a few seconds Morris' voice filled the air. "Surprisingly, Walter is talking with the fat man fifty feet from you and to the right. What's going to surprise you more, is that Mia and Max are not that far from them either. So they might even be able to overhear the conversation. Let me see. Oh, in the meantime, head to your right."

Granny and Pablo instantly moved closer to where Morris said Walter was located. They did not run but moved stealthily, not wanting to scare them, so they maybe could overhear part of the conversation. The fat man and Walter were whispering to each other behind a group of banana trees. Walter's voice rose here and there in a frustrated tone. As Granny glanced through the wide leaves of the banana trees she saw someone else, a woman in her early twenties. She was pretty with dark skin and brown eyes. She was slender, and wore her black hair in a pony tail. She also was adding to the conversation, and her voice was soft, yet compelling. She seemed to take over the conversation, forcing Walter's voice to rise in volume above hers. His hands were on his hips, as he leaned towards the woman, almost threateningly. Then the woman said a few more words and walked away, leaving Walter and the fat man staring after her. Granny was about to come out of her hiding place when she heard Max.

"Hello, Walter," he said and Granny saw him wave at the men. "Have you been waiting long?" Mia was by Max's side. Before they could reach Walter and the fat man, the fat man angled away from him. Granny and Pablo had to lean deeper into the bananas as the fat man walked by them. The fat man didn't noticed them. Granny exhaled the breath she didn't realize she had held. They waited until the fat man was out of sight.

Granny kept her attention on Max and Mia. But the more she stared at them the more her forehead began to furrow. They were filthy. From head to toe, they were covered with mud, dirt, and debris, but Walter didn't seem to notice. He merely answered their question and worked to cover his own actions.

"I've only been waiting a few minutes," he said. "I was talking to some tourists who had lost their way and gave them directions."

"Where's Granny and Pablo?" asked Mia hesitantly. "They were supposed to be with you."

"I . . ." began Walter, but was quickly cut off by Granny, who emerged from the banana grove.

"We're right here, my dears. We've been on the hunt, searching for Walter." She then focused her attention on him. "You worried us when we couldn't find you. Are you all right?" Granny's tone was calm, seemingly filled with concern. She took the hand the creature from the recess had touched.

"I'm fine. Just startled is all. I know I overreacted, but that really creeped me out . . . and I . . . and I panicked."

Granny didn't doubt for one moment that he had panicked. To be honest, she would have done the same thing, except she would have been screaming at the top of her lungs.

"I'm glad you're safe." Granny said, releasing Walter's arm and focused on Max and Mia, but it was Pablo who asked them the next question.

"Where's Spencer?" In the tunnel, Max had waited for Morris to tell them when Emmanuel had gone into the gift shop. Spencer had been able to stall him for five more minutes. Finally, when Spencer was alone, Morris had told Spencer to meet them back by their rooms, that they would get in touch with him soon.

"He was tired and wanted to rest," answered Max as he smiled at Pablo. The answer was good enough for now, but Max knew Pablo would believe there had to be more that wasn't said. The group began to walk towards the Nunnery, when Walter suddenly turned around and confronted Max and Mia.

"Where are your horses?"

Max glanced at Mia, who tried to keep a stone face. He had forgotten all about the fact that they were supposed to be on horses surveying the area.

"You know, we decided to get a little exercise. We left the horses back at the hotel. They were a hindrance anyway. As we were doing research, they kept trying to get away."

Walter stared at Max, clearly not believing him and trying to find a hole in his story. But Max and Mia both smiled at him unwaveringly. So he smiled briefly and nodded.

"I was just curious," he stammered. "That would explain your attire. You both look like you fell in some mud."

They returned to the Nunnery where their horses were tied up. Max and Mia, not able to go back the way they had come, followed behind.

# TWELVE

TWO HOURS HAD PASSED by the time the Crypto-Capers
made it back to the hotel. In the lobby, Spencer joined
them. He was excited, yet concerned about what had
happened to them. The mud on Max and Mia had dried
now, making them look like a beginning pottery students
—or some misguided project such a student had dis-
carded. Max didn't explain his and Mia's appearance,
though Spencer's wide gaze looked them up and down as
he returned Mia's watch to her. Morris would have
briefed him with the basics, including that he had "cho-
sen" to remain behind because he was "tired."

Spencer confirmed Max's story to Pablo as
Morris had coached him. Pablo's features relaxed. They
agreed to get cleaned up and refreshed, then meet for an
early dinner.

Walking down the hallway took a lot of effort for
Max—he was exhausted. When they had gone to the
Nunnery to get the horses, Max had told Granny that he
and Mia could walk, but she would have none of it. Max
had to ride behind Pablo, while Mia had sat behind
Granny. But that didn't eliminate the effort they had

already put into the morning. Max glanced at his appearance through a picture on the wall and noticed how haggard he looked. His gaze swiftly focused on his sister. By Mia's hunched over back and downcast head, he knew she felt the same. The only one who seemed to have energy left was Granny, her quick gait made Max cringe as he tried to keep up.

When the trio reached their door, Max and Mia let Granny open it. When she did, she held it open for them to enter. None of them made it more than three steps into the room. Granny was tucking the key card back in her bag before she looked up, but, when she did, a loud gasp escaped her lips. Their room was in shambles. Someone had torn it apart rather thoroughly.

Without a word, they spread out to see what was missing. "If they were looking for equipment," Max said as he picked up stuff, "they couldn't have taken much. Everything seems to be here. Mia?"

"They went through every item of clothing we had with us," Mia said with disgust, tossing an armful of clothes onto her bed. "My equipment is here, though."

As they moved further into the room, they had to side step more clothes, as well as, bed sheets, pillows, and upturned furniture.

"Who could have done this?" asked Mia as she picked up bits of clothing. "All the suspects were with us or near us at some point, weren't they?"

"I would have thought that to be a true statement," said Max, "but clearly it isn't. If we can figure out what they were looking for, we'd have a shot at figuring out who did this. It's obvious that it had nothing to do with our equipment, though frankly I'm surprised at that."

Then Granny said, "All right, you two, tell me what happened, right down to the smallest detail."

Max filled Granny in, starting with what had happened in the gift shop all the way to the wrong split in the tunnel they took which had led them to an underground mud pit. Mia had fallen into it , and Max had to partially go in and save her. As his story unfolded, Max removed the papers they had found in Emmanuel's office from his backpack, which, thankfully, had not gotten dirty. He handed them to Granny. She perused them briefly, then placed them onto Mia's bed. As she looked up, she noticed that Mia was about to sit down on her bed to rest.

"Don't sit on the bed, dear. You're covered in filth!" Mia glanced down at her appearance and let out a deep sigh. "Why don't you go and take a shower, Mia. Max and I will continue checking the room for evidence before we return things to their normal state." Mia was about to protest, but Granny placed her hands on her hips, her features firm. "Off to the loo with you!"

"Yes, Granny," Mia said gratefully. She grabbed a few of her belongings and picked her way to the bathroom. Granny waited until she heard the water running. Then she slapped her hands together and turned to receive the black powder and brush that Max already had located and was handing her. Then they began dusting for fingerprints, moving from one end of the room to another—dusting and picking up as they went. They were not surprised when they found nothing.

When Mia was done with her shower, she came out and helped with the rest of the clean up, while Max headed to the bathroom. When the room was back to its original order, Granny put away the powder and brush and then glanced at the room with hands on her hips.

"What?" asked Mia.

"I'm just trying to figure out what happened," said Granny as she shook her head and walked over to her backpack, taking something out.

"What's that?"

"I found it when we went searching inside a recess at the Nunnery. I have no clue what it is. I didn't have time to take a picture, so I thought I'd do that now and send it to Morris to look up." Granny snorted loudly as she placed the stone item onto the middle of her newly made bed so she could grab one of her cameras. "I was trying to buy you and Max some time to find what you were looking for, so I started looking at random things to distract everyone. I didn't think I'd actually find something."

Mia plopped down on her bed and dug into her backpack to find a pencil. It immediately got tucked behind her ear. Mia picked up the copies of the cryptograms and studied them. Not quite sure what order they belonged in, she carefully spread them out in front of her and gave them an order. Labeling each top.

## Cryptogram 1

K G T Q    C K Q O    G E E W T Q R    O Q C ?

## Cryptogram 2

D K G C    K G T Q    C K Q O    V H B X R ?

## Cryptogram 3

W X    Y G E H Y G A    C K Q    C E Q G M B E Q

G D G W C M ,    Z B C    X H    M W F X    H V

C G Z A Q C M .

## Cryptogram 4

C K Q O    G E Q    M C G O W X F    G C    G

K H C Q A    W X    Y K W Y K Q X    W C S G

## Cryptogram 5

U W M A Q G R    H B E    V E W Q X R M    D K Q X

I H M M W Z A Q .    B M Q    C K Q    W C Q U

W    M Q X C .

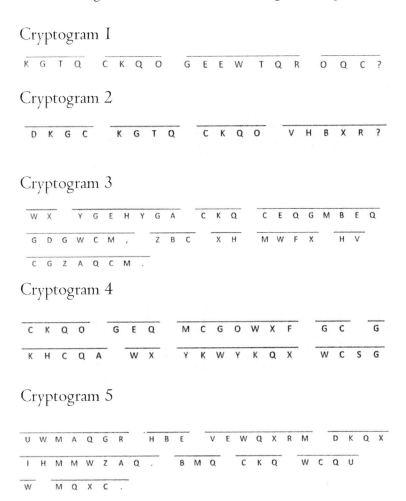

97

Mia then took up the cipher key she had begun to fill in when they had solved the first cryptogram. It wasn't completely filled in, but she had a good start. Using that cipher key, Mia began to solve all of the cryptograms. As each message was revealed, Mia rearranged her original order to make more sense.
(Rearrange your cryptograms to make sense and fill in the new order below.)

Cryptogram 1

_____
_____
_____
_____

Cryptogram 2

_____
_____
_____
_____

Cryptogram 3

_____
_____
_____
_____

Cryptogram 4

_____

_____

_____

_____

Cryptogram 5

_____

_____

_____

_____

As Mia read them aloud, it made her wonder who the person on the receiving end was. She had a feeling who that person was talking to, but who was sending the messages to him? Mia glanced at one of the letters written in Italian.

*Spero queste scoperte di lettera lei bene. So che lei deve avere molte domande, e nella verità, non posso dire voi tutti delle risposte. Con l'attività recente posa lì, non possiamo correre qualunque rischio. Non sono sicuro che che è dopo i nostri cimeli di famiglia, ma procede con l'attenzione. Lei è in grado di aiutare. Ingannare e distrarre quando possibile. Ho bisogno di lei per fare questo per me. So che è molto chiedere, ma lo chiedo di lei. Le pillole e le meridiane non possono essere trovate. A tutto il costo, proteggerli. Viveri sono stati persi a causa di*

*loro, rifiuto di vedere più. Per favore DI capire per-*
*ché non posso dire le la posizione esatta di dove*
*sono nascosti, è per il suo beneficio che faccio non.*
*Non voglio che la sua vita essere distrutta dall'avid-*
*ità come ero, e non la tenterò con le bugie che ho*
*creduto. Se lei ha bisogno di me per niente, sarò lì*
*in un battito di cuore. Tutto l'amore, e sta la cas-*
*saforte.*

Not fluent in that language herself, she did know someone who was. "Granny, could you take a look at these?"

"Sure, dear, I'll be right there." Granny had changed her clothes, freshening up after their long trek. She walked over to Mia's bed and sat down beside her.

"What are you doing?" asked Max as he exited the bathroom, a towel drying off the last bit of wetness from his hair.

"I asked Granny to look over the letters we found."

Max threw the towel into the bathroom before he joined them at Mia's bed. Max and Mia watched with impatience as Granny fiddled with a pencil while she read the first letter. As Granny read, she marked up the paper as needed. Max and Mia were on pins and needles as they waited, leaning forward periodically to catch a glimpse of what Granny was jotting down. When Granny was finished, she pressed the letter to her chest, her features crinkled in thought.

"What? What does it say?" asked Mia.

Granny glanced at the letter and took a deep breath before reading it:

"I hope this letter finds you well. I know you must have many questions, and in truth, I can't tell you all the answers. With the recent activity down there, we cannot take any chances. I am not sure who is after our family heirlooms, but proceed with caution. You are in a position to help. Mislead and distract when possible. I need you to do this for me. I know it is a lot to ask, but I am asking it of you. The tablets and the sundials cannot be found. At all cost, protect them. Lives have been lost because of them. I refuse to see any more. Please understand why I can't tell you the exact location of where they are hidden. It is for your benefit that I don't. I don't want your life to be destroyed by greed as mine was, and I will not tempt you with the lies I believed. If you need me for anything, I will be there in a heartbeat. All my love, and stay safe."

"All my love who?" asked Max.

"The letter is vague on that point," Granny said. "It doesn't say who the letter is from or who it is to."

Max began to pace the room, his hand to his chin in thought.

"And the other letter?" Granny set down the letter she held in her hand and picked up the other. With the

THE LEGEND OF THE GOLDEN MONKEY

same routine, Granny perused the letter and marked it up. After several minutes, she read the translation aloud:

"I think I found an ally to our cause. There is a group here called the Crypto-Capers. They are detectives, not treasure hunters. I have spoken with them. They seem sincere and honest in their intentions. They are after our family heirlooms, but I think they want to protect them. I will talk with them further, and though I have concerns and feel that my position has been compromised, I believe I will be able to resolve them. There are other people who have been asking questions about our heirlooms, people who are not to be trusted. I have been deterring those individuals. They seem determined, but I have a feeling that they are no match for these Crypto-Capers. I do have many questions, but I can see why you cannot tell me everything. Disappointed, I am of course, but I understand. I will protect what is ours regardless. Rest assured, you will not have to come here. I will figure out something."

Max and Mia waited for more, but Granny's adjustment of her glasses and brief smile showed that there was none.

"Is that it?" asked Mia.

"That's it!" exclaimed Granny.

Max pondered the information he had heard. After several minutes, he stopped his pacing and placed his hand on his hips. "We can agree that the Panther was on the receiving end of those cryptograms, can't we?"

"Yes!" replied Granny and Mia in unison.

"But who was sending them?" asked Granny.

"I'm not sure, but I do have a hunch."

"It could have been Walter," said Mia.

"Or the fat man," chimed in Granny.

"Possibly," finished Max. He paused as he thought some more. "What we know for sure is that this is a complicated case, and nothing is what it seems. We were sent down here by Maggie Devereaux to return the artifacts that the Panther had stolen to lure us here, as well as to stop him. Maggie had to have known what the Panther was up to. We know that the Panther is after the tablets and the sundials, which might be used to open the treasure room hidden in the Carocal. The letters that were written confirm that much. We are not treasure hunters, so we could care less on finding the treasure for our own gain, but we do believe in history and want to preserve it.

"Now, if the Panther finds the tablets and the sundials, he'll use them to open the treasure room and take what isn't his. What he thinks is in there and wants so desperately that he's going through all this trouble, is beyond me, though my guess would be this elusive Golden Monkey. It must be what's driving him. With that said, I honestly believe that we might be the only ones who can stop him. The advantage we have is that the Panther doesn't seem to have any clue where the tablets or the sundials are."

"Neither do we," Mia pointed out. "We really don't know who those letters were to or from either."

"We don't . . . and we do," said Max with a smile.

"How's that?" asked Granny.

"Morris, would you care to explain?"

There was a brief pause before Morris's voice emanated from the watch. "Why, thank you, old buddy. I was waiting for my introduction, but first—I have to say—it's impressive, as usual, to hear how your mind works, the way you rationalize things." There was another pause before Morris continued. "The person we're looking for is the same person who pillaged your room looking for one of the pieces. Now, if you'd be so kind as to look over at the computer monitor." The trio moved closer to the monitor. "Max, if you could please."

Max turned the monitor on. Within a few seconds the main screen came up. Then it seemed as if the computer was working by magic. Their web cam page came up and it looked as if a tape was rewinding, which, in reality, it kind of was. Then it stopped and began to play forward again. What they saw was their hotel room.

"Wait for a few moments, and you'll see," started Morris. "I have been playing around with some of the equipment Maggie got for us, and I realized that I'm able to activate your web cam without you being there and without the computer being on. So, I was trying it out, moving the camera all about, when this happened."

They saw their door opening. They all watched in anticipation as they saw someone come into the room and start looking through their belongings. Upon not finding what the person was looking for, he fell on his knees and covered his face with his hands. When he removed them, Max, Mia and Granny, saw who it was.

"That's Emmanuel," said Mia in disbelief. "What could he have been looking for?"

Max immediately walked over to Mia's suitcase and opened her secret compartment. What he removed-he took back to his sister and Granny. "He was looking for these," said Max as he held up the sundials.

"But why?"

"You don't know?" Max's question caused Mia to stare more closely at the sundials.

They seem to look the same, but then Mia noticed the thickness of the one sundial compared to the other, and she pressed her fingertips over her mouth. "Oh, my goodness. The sundials were both on the counter. Emmanuel grabbed back the wrong one, and I took the sundial that Emmanuel had been wearing around his neck! So, that's why you were rushing me out of the shop? You knew what had happened, and you didn't say anything."

Max nodded.

"I'm not okay with that. He treasured his sundial." Mia glared at her brother in frustration.

"He'll get it back, Mia," Max said with a wave of his hand. Then he added more under his breath, "when we are done with it."

Mia punched her brother in the shoulder.

"Your arrogance knows no bounds, Max. For once, could you think of some else's feelings before your own? I'm the one who caused Emmanuel to ransack our room, and, though it proves the sundial's importance, it was still wrong for us to take it from him."

Before Max could reply, Mia folded her arms in front of her chest and turned her back on him. Max glanced at Granny. She didn't look particularly happy either.

Then Morris's face popped up on the monitor. "Frankly, Max, I wouldn't have cared either. Taking the sundial serves our purpose. Emmanuel will get it back, as you said. We aren't treasure hunters, but we do need this piece if we're to solve this mystery."

The trio, stared at the monitor with mixed reactions. Mia glared. Max smiled and nodded in agreement, while Granny sighed and pursed her lips.

"But I do agree that we could have gotten the sundial another way," Morris said quickly.

Max's mouth opened as he heard the kiss up. While Mia and Granny nodded in satisfaction.

"Well," said Morris, "I'm going to get a glass of water now. I'll be listening," then he said more under his breath, "but not imputting." Then his voice became normal again. "Talk to you later." Morris shut off the web cam while Max leaned forward and turned off the monitor.

"Okay, Mia, we'll talk to Emmanuel. We'll try to help him out of the mess we know he's in, but I'm not giving back his sundial until we are done with it."

Mia turned towards her brother. "Thanks for showing at least that smidgen of compassion."

"Yeah, well, don't mention it." Then he said as he turned around and returned the sundials back into Mia's secret compartment. "EVER!"

Granny returned to the bed and sat down. "So, the one letter was from Emmaunel," she said.

"Yes, but we don't know who he was writing to," answered Max.

"The letter was of a personal nature. I'd say it was likely a relative."

"We won't know who exactly unless we get a name to work with," chimed in Morris through the watch phone. "When you talk with him, make sure the question is asked. Then I bet I can figure it out."

"We'll keep that in mind," said Mia as she smiled sweetly at her brother. Max rolled his eyes.

"Did you receive the pictures I took of the item I found, Morris?" asked Granny.

"Yes! I've been running the photos through search programs, but don't have a positive hit yet. I'll keep searching and will let you know when something comes up."

"Thank you, dear."

Max thought a moment. "I think I might know of someone who could tell us about the item." Everyone's attention was focused on Max now. "Mia, I think you know who I'm talking about."

Mia's gaze narrowed on her brother as she thought of who he meant. Then her features relaxed and she smiled. "We need to find Spencer. He'll know what it is. His knowledge of South American artifacts is impressive."

"Go ahead and get him," said Granny. "We'll be waiting."

# THIRTEEN

MIA QUICKLY WALKED FROM THEIR ROOM and into the hallway. Her eyes immediately spotted Spencer's room, which he shared with Pablo and Walter. Mia went to the door and rapped on it. After only a few seconds Pablo opened it, his face breaking into a smile.

"Don't tell me your team is ready to leave again so soon?" Pablo looked tired, and Mia could tell that he had been taking a nap.

"No, not quite yet. Actually, is Spencer around?" Pablo stepped backwards, providing Mia with a look at the inside of their room. Spencer sat in a chair by the glass sliding door, a book in his lap. Mia couldn't tell what the title of it was because as soon as Spencer saw her, he slipped out of the chair to see what she wanted and dropped his book behind him on the seat.

"Hello, Mia. What can I do for you?"

Mia whispered, "Is Walter here?"

Pablo understood what Mia meant and said, "No, he's not. He had to run an errand or something."

"Good! Could you both follow me please?" Mia spun around smoothly on her heel. Pablo and Spencer followed her to her room. Once inside, Max and Granny greeted them. Mia noticed that none of the cryptograms, letters, or the item was in sight.

"What's going on?" asked Pablo curiously.

Granny waited until Mia closed the door before she stood up, the found item in her hands. "Spencer, we need your help with this. I found it when Pablo, Walter, and I were in that tunnel at the Nunnery. We're having a difficult time identifying it, and we thought maybe you might know what it is."

Spencer reached out his hand and gently touched the object. Various squares and rectangles were etched into the top of it. Everyone in the room was waiting with anticipation. After several minutes of studying it, Spencer's features filled with concern.

"This is called a *Yupana*. It is like a calculator and was supposedly used by the Incas. Researchers believed that the calculations were based on Fibonacci numbers to minimize the number of necessary grains per field." Everyone in the room stared at Spencer in amazement. "I saw one at a museum in Peru a few weeks ago."

"Morris!" called Max impatiently.

"I'm on it. Keep your shirt on," replied Morris through the watch phone. Max smiled as he focused on Spencer.

"If you're correct, and this—*Yupana*—is from Peru, what would it be doing here?"

"I can answer that one," started Morris. "The *Yupana was* in a museum in Peru, but was stolen last week. Authorities chased the thief to Machu Picchu, but he was never caught."

"Ah . . . Machu Picchu," sighed Max as he began to pace the length of the room, his hand upon his chin in thought. "The Spanish conquered everyone. They overtook the Mayans, the Aztecs, and the Incas, plundering the villages, taking what they wanted. Much of native history was destroyed during their years of conquering."

"Yes," said Spencer, "but remember, Machu Picchu is also different from the other cities. It was the only one that could have defeated the Spanish. That, and the Spanish never found it."

Max whipped around and focused his attention on Spencer. The rest of the team did as well.

"You mentioned that before when we had first met you," stated Mia.

"I mention it again because it's very important and needs to be remembered," answered Spencer.

"Refreshen our memories!" insisted Granny.

"The Incan communities were built high in some of the Andes Mountains. To make travel easier over the deep river gorges, the Incas erected suspension bridges. These bridges were used to get people from one village to the other. They were made of twisted ropes made of plants—such as grass or vines—and lasted for hundreds of years. Some scholars believed that if the Incas would have cut those ropes, the suspension bridges would have prevented the Spanish from defeating the Incas."

"I still find that information interesting. What of the other thing you mentioned?" asked Granny.

"The Spanish never found the elusive village of Machu Picchu. It was pretty high up. Because of this, much of its history is still intact. Machu Picchu was thought to be a type of training place for priestesses and noble women. Scholars' views have changed over the years though, and they now think that Machu Picchu could have been used as a royal or religious retreat. Either way, it's a phenomenal place. It had agricultural terraces and fresh water from springs. It also had bathhouses, palaces, storage rooms, temples, and astrological structures, along with about one hundred and fifty houses—which were all made of granite blocks. It's quite impressive."

"Astrological structures, you say?" asked Max.

"Yes!"

"Like—sundials?"

Spencer narrowed his gaze and nodded.

"Of course! Just like the rest of the Central and South American civilizations, the Incas worshipped the sun and believed heavily in astronomy. As the Spanish swept through the region, they knew this and destroyed all the sundials, except one."

"The one at Machu Picchu," said Max. "I knew it! I KNEW IT!" The arrogant smile on Max's lips and the confidence in his step clearly indicated he had solved something.

"What do you think is going on then?" asked Mia.

"The thief, Morris," Max said. "In the research you've done, was there a name or anything that revealed him?"

"No," answered Morris firmly. "But I think I know where you're going with this."

"Enlighten us, please," encouraged Granny.

"Well, if we're thinking on the same page here, I'd say that the Panther, or one of his many accomplices, stole the artifact Granny found in Peru and went to Machu Picchu looking for the sundial, somehow knowing that it would be intact."

Max nodded emphatically.

"After that," continued Morris, "I'm not quite sure what else could have happened."

"Well done, mate. We're on the same page here. I also think that the Panther knows about the sundial. When we looked at the Carocal, I noticed places where a small sundial could fit, just like the one Emmanuel had. I'll bet you there's another location for a sundial on top the ruin where the sun could hit it to open the vault. Now, the Panther must have figured out that to a point, which was why he went to Machu Picchu—it was to see how the other sundial was set up and, if it was small enough, to steal it.

"Now, at the risk of almost getting caught, he takes the *Yupana* and leaves it here for us to find. That it was planted here, I know for sure. What I don't know is *who* precisely did it. Not having all the information he needs, the Panther is using us again to unravel things for him. It's amazing to me how often he needs our help. It must burn him to feel he needs us." Max began to laugh and pace.

Mia leaned to Spencer's ear. "Max does this all the time. It's his way of ferreting things out. When he's like this, he looks a little daft, but he does come up with some pretty interesting ideas," Mia whispered.

Spencer turned to Mia and smiled. Then they both focused their attention back on Max.

"I just had a disturbing thought," interrupted Morris. "Do you think the Panther knows about Emmanuel?"

"Oh, sure. That's why he's been using him as a go-between. Emmanuel knows Italian and can speak Spanish and English. He works where he can easily receive and interpret information."

"But how is he getting the info?" asked Mia.

Max shrugged and continued to pace.

Morris said, "Through his fax machine. Didn't you see that one in his office? E-mails are too traceable as are cell phones, though there are ways to get around that. And though a fax machine's number can be traced, what's actually faxed cannot."

"That makes sense," said Mia. "Now what?"

"Well, I think the Panther will assume that we'll leave Chichen Itza and head for Machu Picchu to return the artifact to its rightful owners and to study the area. He's trying to get us out of the way for something, and I bet it has everything to do with Emmanuel."

"We must protect Emmanuel, Max. We can't let the Panther have him," said Spencer.

"I can alert the authorities and have him protected," offered Pablo.

Max stopped and held out his hand. "No, Pablo, we need him as bait."

Granny put her hands on her hips. "He is not a piece of meat, Maxwell. I refuse to feed him to that wolf. Besides, we can't use him without his consent. He must know the danger he's going to be in." When Max's expression didn't change, she added, "You want to put Emmanuel's life in danger just to catch the notorious Panther? Risk his life to catch a fool?"

Max frowned. "He may be a fool, but he's a fool who'll find another way to catch Emmanuel if we don't do it this way." Max's tone was unmistakably determined.

Granny shook her head several times again in disapproval.

"What are we going to do?" asked Mia.

"We're going to head for Machu Picchu."

Mia scowled. "No! We can't leave Emmanuel when he needs us the most."

"We must and we will! With us out of the way, the Panther will have one of his accomplices come after Emmanuel. I'm sure of it. They'll need him to reveal where the tablets are."

Mia narrowed her eyes. "But we know Emmanuel doesn't know where they are."

"That's to our advantage, isn't it?"

Spencer took a step towards Max. "But he'll be alone. He'll be unprotected."

Max rolled his eyes and made a raspberry. "The last thing he'll be is alone or unprotected." With that, Max loosened the watch on his wrist and handed it to Spencer. "We'll meet with him and give him that. Set up a time for us to consult. We're depending on your friendship with Emmanuel to help us."

Spencer obviously was conflicted. Clearly, he had reservations, but he was also fairly vibrating with excitement as he clenched the watch in his fist. "You can depend on me," Spencer said proudly.

Max smiled. "I knew we could."

"What would you like me to do?" asked Pablo.

Max glanced at Granny for support. After a moment, her whole demeanor changed as some realization dawned on her. "You'll need to spread the word that we'll be leaving tomorrow morning. Make sure you're overheard, especially by that tourist group that hangs out in the lobby. We'll also need you to make preparations for us to fly to Machu Picchu. Can it be done?"

Pablo squared his shoulders. "Of course. I own two planes. One is always ready to fly in a pinch."

"Good, because we'll need them both," she said.

Pablo wasn't sure what Granny meant, but he nodded anyway. "It shall be done."

Max clasped his hands together and finally stopped pacing. "Excellent, and remember, make sure you're overheard by lots of people. No matter what, you need to create a stir! Now, let's get moving. We each know what we have to do."

Max's words were electric. Though little of the plan had been voiced, everyone seemed to know what they had to do and hurried to do it. The group split up, each tending to his or her facet of the gambit.

# FOURTEEN

THAT DAY WAS CHAOTIC. Though much had to be done, each piece of the game was put into play.

Max was sitting in the back of Pablo's jeep, his hand shielding him from the blinding effects of the early morning sun as he glanced back at the caravan of jeeps trailing behind. Their plan had worked out perfectly— too perfectly. Directly behind Pablo's jeep was Walter. Behind him was the fat man, and in his jeep were some of his tourist group friends. When Pablo had spoken of their departure, he also offered plane service to anyone who wished to take a trip to Machu Picchu.

Dust from the vehicles filled the air creating a thick fog through the jungle as the result of that offer. The key players were lining up, and now Max felt as if he were playing chess.

As Max turned forward again, he could see the airstrip ahead. His gaze quickly moved to Mia, who was sitting next to him, her features solemn. Spencer was sitting on the other side of her, his gaze focusing out the window. In the back seat Granny chatted wildly, her hands moving as fast as her lips. When the jeeps entered the air field and pulled alongside the planes, Max's heart began to beat fast. After taking several deep breaths, he got out of the jeep, leaving the door open for Mia and Spencer.

Max and everyone in his group went to the back of their jeep to remove their bags. Max, Mia, and Granny put their backpacks over their shoulders as they held fast to the rest of their belongings, pulling them behind them. They followed Pablo and Spencer as they made their way to the second plane. He watched as the other jeeps pulled up and began unloading, except they headed for the first plane, which was bigger than the second so it could hold more people.

Mia followed her group up the stairs and into the plane. They sat and got comfortable, while Pablo closed the door behind them and moved to the cockpit with Spencer. She listened to the conversation Pablo was having with the tower as well as with Walter. Then their engine roaring loudly. Pablo and Spencer began their checks. Soon they could hear Walter's plane as it took off in front of them. Then their plane began to move slowly to position itself on the runway.

For the first time in his flying career, Pablo was nervous. Not about flying, but of what was about to unfold. After taking several deep breaths, he closed his eyes and said a prayer. Spencer looked at his brother, his confidence in what they were doing strongly in his eyes. Spencer gave his brother a smile and said in a firm voice, "We're a go!"

After taking several more deep breaths, Pablo put his mind to the task. The plane picked up speed, and soon they were speeding down the runway. Then the bumpy ride smoothed out as they lifted off the ground. The plane gained its balance, and they rose smoothly over the magnificent jungle with the Mayan ruins in the background, and followed the plane already only a speck in front of them, winging south and west to the Andes Mountains and whatever lay in their future.

# FIFTEEN

EMMANUEL WAS SITTING in the gift shop office, the shop unlocked but the sign still saying closed. He knew that, at that very moment, the Crypto-Capers were flying away from him. He was nervous about what was to come. When he'd met with the Crypto-Capers, they'd told him what to expect, and yet it didn't make him feel any better. He quickly glanced at the watch Spencer had given him. He didn't know how a watch could save him, but he was willing to give anything a try.

He locked the papers he considered important in a file drawer. When that was done, he checked to make sure he wasn't leaving any evidence for someone else to find, then he rested his face in his hands. He had been under a great deal of stress for a very long time.

The phone rang. Emmanuel's heart nearly leapt from his chest. He was about to grab it, when he realized that it was his fax machine. Within seconds, a piece of paper fed out from the bottom. Emmanuel grabbed it and looked at what it said.

**RUN!**

Without hesitation, Emmanuel pressed the button on the desk that opened the secret passageway. As he got up and was running to the passage, he heard the tinkling of the gift shop doorbell. Fear drove him into the opened passageway. But as he glanced to the right, he noticed some things he knew had not been there before. As he reached for the flashlight hanging on the wall, he quickly closed the passageway door. His heart was thumping. As the door locked into place, he glanced one more time at the paper in his hand, every fiber of his being tingling. He couldn't help but wait a few minutes, curious if everything Max had said could possibly be correct, but then he heard it. A loud yell came from the other side of the wall. "NOOOOOOOO!"

At that moment Emmanuel's legs were set in motion, and he ran, hoping that whoever was in the office didn't know how to open the secret door and wouldn't figure it out quickly. He ran after the bouncing light of his flashlight until he was far away from the door, deep into the convoluted tunnels. His legs were tired and achy, but he didn't stop. When the path forked, he took the tunnel to the right, a passage he knew would take him to the main road.

Once he left the tunnel system, he crouched, panting and sweating, among a thick growth of ferns and young banana plants, sheltered among the trunks of some fig trees. Emmanuel was scared. He didn't want to leave the safety of the undergrowth, but then he saw it, the brightly colored bus he knew took tourists around the island, and this one seemed to be heading back towards the Riveria Maya. With courage he wasn't sure was in him, Emmanuel stepped from his hiding place and moved to the edge of the road. He hastily shook his arm to get the driver's attention. When the man saw him, he stopped the bus. Emmanuel got on and sat in a seat towards the back.

The bus began to wheeze into motion again, and Emmanuel sighed in relief, a few tears pushing from his eyes. He tried to be courageous, but he felt he was failing misereably as he began to shake. Then, out of nowhere, a voice came to him. "You're doing well, Emmanuel. Hang in there. You'll get through this."

Emmanuel glanced around him, but all the gaudily dressed tourists were chatting amongst themselves or looking out the windows. There was no one close enough to talk to him. Then he heard the voice again. It radiated from the watch. "I'm here to help you."

"And who are you?" asked Emmanuel tentatively.

"A friend! Can you talk?"

Emmanuel stared at the people in front of him and knew it wasn't safe. "No!" he whispered harshly.

"Find a place where we can talk in private, then call me."

"How can I do that?" whispered Emmanuel, his eyes darting all around.

"Just talk. I'll hear you."

After that, the watch grew silent. Emmanuel waited anxiously as the bus lumbered along the road. In town, Emmanuel hopped off and walked to the beach, finding a quiet spot where he wasn't surrounded by people. He sat on the warm white sand and looked out at the ocean. The longer he sat, the more the humid air coiled itself around him, settling on his sweating body. Now, more than ever, the temptation to jump and lose himself in the oceans depths enveloped him, but he denied the urge. Instead, he raised his arm and spoke into the watch. "Umm . . . I'm here," began Emmaunel, unsure of if the person on the other side could hear him. "Hello?"

"I'm listening, Emmanuel. I'm here."

"Could you tell me what's going on please? My life is in danger."

"I know," began the voice. "Are you sure you can't be overheard?" Emmaunel again looked around him. A few children were playing in the water off to his left, and far to his right an older couple, walking hand in hand, headed away from him. Other than that, he was alone. It was quiet, except for the soothing, rhythmic splash and splosh of the waves rolling interminably onto the beach and withdrawing as mysteriously as they had come.

"No one can hear us."

"What about those kids in the water?"

"No, they are too far a—" Emmanuel gaped at the children and then at the watch. "How did you know?" Then he said, "Who are you?"

"My name is Morris, and I'm one of the Crypto-Capers. I'm the computer person of the group, and, though I'm not physically beside you, believe me when I say that I can see you and pretty much what's around you.

I want to assure you that I'm trustworthy and devoted to my team. I care about their well being and safety. And yours. Above all else, know that I'm here to help you. The watch on your wrist is a way to me. You were given the watch so I could help you. Do you understand?"

The question was absurd. Believe in a watch? No, the watch was not who he believed in, but he was starting to believe in Morris. The tightening in his chest seemed to ease with Morris's reassurance.

"I want to trust you, Morris, but . . ."

"I'm sure that perfidy is a thing common in your life, especially with what you know, but I assure you again, I'm not here to hurt you, and I won't betray your trust."

Emmanuel thought over Morris's words for several minutes, thought about Max and Mia and Spencer, then made a decision. "I believe that you can help me, Morris. What should I do?"

"First, I need to know more about who sent you that letter?"

At first, Emmanuel was unsure of what Morris was talking about, then it hit him. "You want to know about the tablets, don't you?"

"And the sundials."

Emmanuel scoffed. "You have one of them, so I'm sure you know what it can do."

"Mia didn't realize she'd taken it. She was surprised when Max told her she had, but yes, it's in our possession. You know this because you tore up my team's hotel room looking for it. Believe me when I say that we don't want the treasure, and upon the completion of this case, you'll have the sundial returned to you. We want to protect the treasure from the person who does want it."

"And who is that?" asked Emmanuel.

"I can't tell you who the person behind everything is. I don't know. But if we hadn't helped you already, he would've had no issue hurting you to get what he needed. We know you don't know where the tablets are, and we also know that the person who sent you that letter written in Italian is a relative. What can you tell me about the letter?"

Emmanuel's jaw had dropped at how much Morris knew about him, when all this time he'd thought he'd been so secretive.

"I need to know some history, Emmanuel."

"My grandfather wrote the letter."

"Is your grandfather Dante De Luca?" Morris's tone was hopeful. If Dante was Emmanuel's grandfather, then everything happening was making sense.

Again Emmanuel was shocked. "Yes, Dante is my grandfather. The tablets have been in our family for years, and now it's my duty to protect them. My grandfather often told me that his life was turned around by the treasure, but not in a good way. My grandfather and his brother Marcello found it years ago when they were in their prime and had come to Chichen Itza to look for their fortune. They were driven by desire for that treasure. My grandfather said that he felt as if it had been calling him. He even had dreams about it.

126

"They found the tablets and the sundials during their adventures. But when the day came to finally be able to open the treasure room, something wasn't quite right. My grandfather said they should do more research, maybe visit Machu Picchu and do more figuring. You see, my grandfather believed that there was a certain way to position the sundials to open the room. The Incas were the only other culture to still have a sundial intact. So he wanted to study that culture more, but Marcello wouldn't hear of it.

"When they opened the room, it was empty. And when I say empty, I mean nothing was in the room except dirt and cobwebs. Not even broken pottery remained, which told my grandfather that they had done something wrong. There was another way to open the room to reveal the one with the treasure, but Marcello didn't believe him. What happened that day caused anger and mistrust between the brothers. Their lives were never the same.

"Then my grandfather met my grandmother, Caterina, and they fell in love. But Marcello fell in love with her too. This caused more problems between them. My grandmother, not wanting to create even more of a drift between the brothers, and yet not wanting to lose the love of her life, made a decision. She chose my grandfather over his brother. In doing so, Marcello's hatred of my grandfather was complete. Then one day, the situation came to a head, as my grandfather knew that it would. Marcello asked him to meet him at the top of the main temple of Chichen Itza. He flew down here and met him. They argued. The entire time my grandfather was begging Marcello for forgiveness, not wanting to continue with the discord between them.

"But Marcello was a self-absorbed man and greedy. He was jealous of my grandfather, who had everything Marcello wanted, except for the treasure, which he still blamed my grandfather for not finding. Then my grandmother showed up. She climbed the mighty steps of the temple in an attempt to bring peace to the brothers, but little did she know that she was going to be one of the casualties." Emmanuel's voice paused briefly as he licked his lips. Morris's attention was focused on every word.

"My grandmother began yelling at the two of them, chastising them for their foolishness. Marcello was so angry with my grandfather that he threw one of the tablets at his head. My grandfather caught it, but not before it scratched his right cheek, leaving a permanent disfigurement. Blood gushed from the wound, but that didn't stop him. My grandfather lunged towards his brother, and they fought. Closer and closer they came to the edge of the platform, and then it happened.

"Marcello was seething with hatred. My grandfather said that it had consumed him, changing him into someone he didn't recognize. Marcello rushed forward, his plan was to knock my grandfather off of the top, but my grandfather side stepped. Realizing to late what his fate was going to be, Marcello reached out and grabbed my grandmother's arm, and they both sailed over the side. There was nothing that my grandfather could do, except watch his brother and his wife roll down the stairs of the temple and land in a heap of broken bones at the bottom.

"By the time he reached them, they were both dead. He said that he wept more than the floods sent by God. Even though it has been years since the tragic event happened, my grandfather still recalls it. He said he will never forget it." Emmanuel's eyes filled with tears.

"The pain he had to endure," began Morris.

"You see now why he had to hide the tablets?" Emmanuel said quickly. "You understand now why he did what he did? My grandfather didn't want the same fate for someone else."

Morris's voice came through the phone. "Your story reminds me of the legend of the two prince brothers, your grandfather being the good brother and Marcello being the evil one."

"My grandfather has said that his life mirrored that story in many ways. In his house there are many unique things. I have been there only a few times. He keeps a painting of a Chechen tree in his living room to remind him of Marcello. If you remember the tale of the brothers, then you'll remember that the evil brother comes back as that. I think my grandfather hopes that its presence will somehow rectify what was done. For my grandmother, he keeps a beautiful white flower, and when it starts to wilt, he quickly replaces it with another. At times I have caught him staring at, caressing its petals. He becomes rather melancholy after that."

"I admire your devotion to your family, Emmanuel," Morris said. "I'm curious though. Where is your grandmother and Marcello buried?"

Emmanuel thought for a moment. "They're both buried in Italy. My grandfather makes a ritual of visiting their graves. I've seen them. But my grandfather wanted to leave something down here to remember him by, since Marcello was so obsessed with this place, so he had a large stone engraved with his name planted in the Xel-Ha park."

"What is Xel-Ha park?"

"It's an amazing natural wonder. Think of it as a large aquarium, really, except that you can actually swim with some of the fish, including dolphins."

Morris was quiet a few moments, then he said, "Emmanuel, I know where your grandfather hid the tablets. Can you go to Xel-Ha park today?"

A little confused, Emmanuel said, "Of course. It's open now."

"Good! Take a taxi. When you get to the park, I'll walk you through it and tell you exactly where you need to go."

"I've been there before, Morris. I know how to get to the Chacah Garden. I've seen the stone with Marcello's name on it many times."

"Good, then you can lead me through it. Go now! I'll be keeping an eye on you."

"Thanks Morris!" Emmanuel rose from the warm white sand, dusted his clothing off and walked towards the road. There were many taxis waiting for tourists. Emmanuel picked one, got in, and soon it drove off. Morris could see what was happening by satellite. He maneuvered his camera to get a healthy look at the taxi's license plate, then zoomed out.

BEING TIRED FROM ALL of the activity, Morris's mind reeled with all of the information he had been given. He leaned back in his chair, raised his long arms above his head and stretched. After he lowered his arms, he moved his neck to one side, then the other, to stretch it. Feeling suddenly parched, Morris stood from his chair to get a glass of water. As he looked around him, he noticed the messiness of his surroundings. He had made camp at the Holmes' residence as usual, and, as usual, it was a mess. However, he did keep one room clean—surprisingly.

Morris had created a secret space off of the living room where all of their secrets would be safe. It was a little room hidden in the walls that contained all of their computer hardware, printers, fax machines, scanners, a chemistry set with test tubes and beakers connected to a computer, as well as some high-tech equipment, and anything else one could imagine. Maggie Devereaux had helped Morris get some of the things they needed for the room and also put him in contact with some great workers to help him make it without it being obvious to someone coming into the house. But she wasn't the only one to help; actually, he'd gotten assistance from his own government. A favor for a favor, it was called. Morris helped many people around the world with little favors, which always paid off for his team in the end. Now the room was almost completed, and if he did it right, the room would be nearly impenetrable from intruders. That, and have everything they would ever need to solve any case.

Morris was about to go to the kitchen for some food and a beverage, when he noticed something. The picture on the computer screen was still showing the place where Emmanuel's taxi had been. Stepping into the street and looking in the direction where the taxi had gone was someone unexpected. Morris immediately slid back into his chair in front of his computer and zoomed in on the picture. He watched as the person brought out a picture and stared at it. Morris zoomed in on the picture the best he could. When the camera focused, Morris was staring at a picture of Emmanuel.

Then the person moved hastily to a taxi nearby, got in and took off. Thinking that was all the excitement he was going to get, a loud, "BEEP!" sounded from his computer. Morris's fingers moved with haste on the keyboard as the screen he had been watching for weeks came up. It was a sight he was dreading to see.

# SIXTEEN

EMMANUEL'S TAXI DROPPED HIM off at the main entrance. Xel-Ha park was enormous and beautiful, full of natural wonders. Every time Emmanuel came to it, he felt like Indiana Jones on one of his adventures. All he needed was the hat and the whip.

Emmanuel quickly queued in one of the lines and paid his entrance fee. After receiving his ticket, he entered and raised his hand casually, as if scratching his chin. "Morris, I'm in."

Morris didn't answer. Emmanuel tried again, his heart starting to race from his anxiety. "Morris!"

"I'm here. Don't worry, but you need to move with haste. You have a tail."

"What?" said Emmanuel, and he turned and looked at the crowd entering the park behind him. "I saw him near the beach. He had your picture."

"Who is it?"

"I don't really know. The face was covered by a hat. I am working on it. I do know what the person was wearing, though, so I'll keep an eye out for that, okay? Now, where are we going?"

"Do you have a map?" asked Emmanuel curiously.

"That all depends on what kind of map you're talking about?" started Morris. "From where I'm sitting, I can see the park from above. It's better than any paper map."

"Well, we need to go past the dolphin's inlet." Emmanuel began to move as he talked softly to Morris. The dolphin tank was always a big attraction. A few tourists were in the tanks swimming with the dolphins, and many were taking pictures and waving. Emmanuel smiled as he remembered when he had done the very same thing. The experience would always bring a smile to his lips.

"I'm now walking towards the restaurant area and the beach. That will take us to the other side more quickly. It's a short cut."

Emmanuel didn't make contact with Morris again until he was in front of a bridge. As he began to cross it, he said, "I'm now walking on a bridge near a swimming area."

"Is anyone around you?" asked Morris.

"No, just me. Can you truly see me?" Emmaunel glanced up, not quite sure what he was looking at.

"Of course, I've been tracking you since

you got there. Wave!" Emmanuel began to wave. "Right hand!" Emmanuel lowered his hand and laughed.

"The trail in front of me is where we need to go. It'll lead us to the Chacah Garden."

"Then let's move with haste. Your tail just entered the park." Emmanuel looked behind him instinctively. What he was expecting to see, he wasn't sure.

"I'm not used to working under so much pressure," moaned Emmanuel.

"Buck up, mate. I do so all the time. I live under a tremendous amount of pressure, but you can do this. Plus, you have me to help you, so you'll be fine. Just remember that the person after you has to follow your same path to get to you and that's if they know where you're going, which at this point, I don't think is true. The person is taking the long way around, which tells me many things. Just make it to the garden and focus on your task. Go!"

Emmanuel moved as if a fire had been lit underneath him. It didn't take him long to make it to the garden. He waited patiently for some tourists to move on to another site before moving between the trees. Emmanuel was nervous as his eyes searched for Marcello's name, remembering where it was located. He found it quickly and rushed to kneel in front of it.

"Morris, I'm here. I'm looking at Marcello's stone."

"Has the ground around the spot been touched?"

"No! It looks the same way as it did the last time I was here."

"Good, now, find something to dig with—quickly."
Emmanuel searched around him until he found a flattened rock. "I found a rock," said Emmanuel.

"First class, mate, we have it just in case we need it. Try lifting the edge of the stone. I'm curious to see if the tablets are hidden underneath it." When Emmanuel touched the stone Morris blurted quickly, "Is the stone, thick or thin?"

"Thick!"

"Aaaah! We may not need the rock. Hurry, lift the stone. Lift! Lift!"

Urgency permeating Morris's every word, Emmanuel dug his fingers into the ground at the base of the stone nameplate, trying to lift it. It took him several times, his fingernails filling with dirt for his efforts. The sun was warm, beating down on him relentlessly during his task, but he was finally able to lift it. Emmanuel looked into the dark hole.

"Do you want me to dig, Morris?"

"Tell me what you see first."

"I see dirt."

"Wow, your description is incredible." Morris's tone was filled with sarcasm.

"All right! I see dark, somewhat, damp dirt."

"Better, now check the underside of the stone," Morris's voice directed.

Emmanuel looked at the underside of the stone and was surprised to see a rectangular piece set into it. "I think I see it, Morris. I see one of the tablets."

"Just one. Not both of them?" Morris's tone was hopeful.

"No, just the one."

"Can you remove it?"

Emmanuel pried at it with his fingers, but it didn't come free.

"Do you have a Leatherman or something?"

"A what?" asked Emmanuel.

"A retractable knife! Something?"

"You know, I'm not like your team that has everything and the kitchen sink in their backpack. But I do happen to carry a knife with me. Hang on!" Emmanuel searched in his left side pocket. "Yes, here it is."

"Try to finagle the tablet out, would you?"

Emmanuel worked his knife between the tablet and the stone. It took him about ten minutes, but he was finally able to do it. "I got it!" Emmanuel shouted with excitement.

"Tell me, what does it have on it?"

Emmanuel turned the tablet over, and sure enough, on the stone piece was a carving of a jaguar.

"A jaguar!"

"Yes!" Morris shouted excitedly. "It's one of the tablets. Now, replace the stone nameplate and get out of there. Try to make the ground look untouched."

Emmanuel did what he was told and replaced the stone nameplate, trying not to disturb the ground around it anymore than he had too. He then held tablet tightly within his grasp and pressed it against his chest.

He turned around and peered out through the trees. The tablet felt heavy and cold. The weight of it embodied the promise that Emmanuel had made, and his determination to keep it. After readjusting his grip, he was about to step out onto the dirt path but was suddenly pushed back through the trees by a slender hand.

Stepping towards him was a woman with dark chestnut hair and pretty features. He noticed that she was not wearing a hat. "Excuse me, miss. I didn't see you." Emmanuel tried to move around the woman, but she pushed him again.

"You'll be going nowhere, Emmanuel. Not until I get what I came here for." The woman paused as she stared at the tablet in Emmanuel's hands. "The tablet, if you please."

"No! I won't give it to you." Suddenly, Emmanuel began to fill with courage. He stood fast, and he tightened his grip on the tablet. "You'll have to take it from me."

The woman's smile was charming and yet determined. "So be it!" She then removed a pistol from her jacket and pointed it towards Emmanuel. "The tablet, please!" Her other arm extended to receive the stone.

Emmanuel grew furious. "I won't let you have it. You don't understand what it can do. The pain this piece of stone can cause. I—"

"I don't care, boy. What I care about is how much I'm going to get paid for delivering it. So, you leave me no choice."

The woman cocked her pistol, aimed it towards Emmanuel, who didn't flinch, and—POW! That was the sound Emmanuel heard as the woman in front of him crumpled to the ground in a heap.

"WH—WHAT?" was all that Emmanuel could say as he watched Granny crack her knuckles in front of him. Max and Mia were standing by her side, smiling. Emmanuel stared. "How did—? What are you—?" he said again more softly.

Mia stepped over and placed her hand on Emmanuel's shoulder. "We're so proud of you. You were so brave."

Emmanuel was in shock. His grip on the tablet loosened as Mia took hold of it, easing it from his grasp. She looked at it quickly before handing it to Max, who glanced at it briefly before placing it into his backpack.

Granny knelt down beside the woman on the ground and tied her hands using a zip tie. She then removed the fingerprint scanner from her backpack, placed the woman's index finger on the pad and scanned it. When it was finished she said, "Morris, trace this will you?"

"Before I do, we are in some deep jelly."

"What?" asked Granny as she stood.

"We have a new problem. Take one guess who has joined the game?" Max glanced at Mia, who glanced at Granny, who raised her hands to her mouth.

"Kris Angel, that wild and crazy magician?"

"Wishful thinking—but no. You need to move and right now. The Panther is loose in the park and is on the prowl."

Max reached out and grabbed Emmanuel, tugging him along as they ran from Chacah's Gardens out onto the dirt path.

"Where is he?"

"On your left. Coming up fast. The woman was a decoy, a distraction. We knew this would happen."

"Yes, but I was hoping it wouldn't." Max led the way as they turned right and hastily moved towards the bridge. Max only glanced a few times behind him, but Granny urged him not too. Soon enough they heard a loud yell, one that was too familiar. It was one of anger and possible defeat. The sound drove them forward, urging them into a run.

"Do you see him?" shouted Max excitedly as he propelled Emmanuel forward.

"He's trying to figure out which way you went. The woman is beside him. Run, Max! Don't worry about what the Panther's doing. Run!"

The group continued until they made it out of the park. Waiting for them in the parking lot was Pablo and Spencer. They had taken over a taxi, and Pablo was behind the wheel.

"Come on!" Pablo shouted from the lowered window, his hand urging them to hurry. The group immediately ran to the taxi and dove in. Pablo stepped on the gas and sped off.

# SEVENTEEN

IN THE TAXI, MAX had pressed his hand over his eyes trying to think, his heart beating loudly in his chest.

"What's our next move?" asked Pablo, his heart racing fast as if they had just robbed a bank and the police were chasing after them.

Max shook his head. "Morris, where do we stand?"

"Thankfully, on two legs. You took a gamble, mate, but it paid off. The Panther's still wandering through the park, running from his own demons. The police we sent after him will keep him busy for hours. Right now he has no clue what just happened, no clue that we set him up. He's probably pretty upset by the fact that we had outsmarted him again. How you knew he would take the bait is beyond me. I personally didn't think he would. In fact, I was positive that he'd send another accomplice to fetch the tablet for him."

"Which he did!" chimed in Mia.

"That reminds me," started Morris through the watch phone. "The woman's name is Marissa Sanchez. She has several warrants out for her arrest. Her latest warrant was for stealing artifacts in South America."

The group pondered this new information for only a few seconds.

"The Panther chooses his accomplices well. He sent more than just one this time to deter us," added Granny.

"That's not entirely true," piped in Pablo, "but you knew that, didn't you, Max?" Pablo's eyes, through the rear view mirror focused on Max.

"I know Maggie Devereaux. She sent us down here for a reason. She's a smart lady."

"What are you talking about?" asked Mia. There was a brief pause. Pablo was going to answer the question, but Emmanuel had figured it out. "Walter is CIA. For weeks he's been coming to me and my father for information. I've been passing on information from him. Unlike the fat man, I had to destroy Walters's messages in front of him, so, other than what I read, I have nothing to trace back to him. He was clever on that point. But as you know, I kept the fat man's correspondence. His interested me the most."

"You poor, dear," said Granny sympathetically.

"Maggie knew that Walter was down here snooping around after the disappearance of the Mayan artifacts, but she also knew that your team could outsmart him," explained Pablo.

"That was why she wouldn't answer me when I asked her why she couldn't involve the CIA," said Max candidly. "They were already involved."

"You're right, Max. Maggie knew much more than what she had confided in you. The truth is, the CIA has a stake in the Panther as well. Lots of people around the world want a piece of him. With the price on his head, well, the CIA's involvement shouldn't be a surprise to anyone," continued Pablo.

"What of the fat man?" asked Mia. "Who is he?"

"He is one of the Panther's accomplices. We used Walter to get him out of the way. When Walter first joined me, I had no clue of his true identity. We're friends, but it wasn't until recently that I found out he was CIA."

Granny shook her head and clucked her tongue. "I worry that the Panther will eventually figure things out and catch us in our own deception."

"One day he will, Granny. The Panther's a smart man, and one with means, but we played our roles well. He thought we went to Machu Picchu. He had no reason not to believe that. Thinking that Emmanuel would be alone, he sent this woman after him, another accomplice, but he came down here for added measure, believing he was close to what he wants. He thought he'd find both tablets, thought he'd be able to open the treasure room as soon as he did. As we know, he was quite mistaken. I believe he thought his quest would be easier than what it is. I don't think he anticipated what truly happened. The Panther is a man who doesn't do all of his homework. He had pieces of the puzzle but filled in the gaps with what he thought he knew."

"He underestimated Emmanuel's grandfather," said Morris through the watch. "Which surprises me because

Dante is a complex man who wouldn't put his eggs all in one basket. No, that's not Dante De Luca at all."

"You would know, Morris," muttered Max more to himself, then he raised his voice, saying more loudly, "Where do we go from here? I'm almost out of ideas."

"Emmanuel, why don't you tell us where we need to go next?" encouraged Morris.

Emmanuel knew what to say but wasn't sure how he felt about it. The whole day had been a roller coaster ride he wished would end. It amazed him how he had been used and the truth of everything. He felt cross and frustrated, then elated and relieved. Suddenly, Spencer reached out and patted Emmanuel on the knee.

"You are alive, Emmanuel, and you were very brave. You did what you had to do. Don't doubt yourself on that."

Emmanuel looked up and gave Spencer a weak smile. "I feel like such a fool." He had the attention of everyone in the taxi now. "And yet I somehow feel relieved that it is finally over."

"It is not over yet, dear," added Granny. "It isn't over until we are away from here. Until then we'll have to keep looking over our shoulders to see if the Panther's following us."

The occupants of the taxi grew quiet, and, out of instinct, each of them looked out the back window.

"If you wish to find the other tablet, you'll need to go see my grandfather," Emmanuel said softly as he closed his eyes.

"I tried that, Emmanuel, but he denied me his attention, dismissing me, and I wasn't the only one," responded Morris grumpily. Emmanuel's features calmed, his eyes focusing on the headliner of the taxi. "Well, Morris, I believe you'll have his full attention now, don't you?" Emmanuel's words held a double meaning

"We will indeed," inserted Max quickly as he placed his hand tightly on his backpack where he knew the tablet lay peacefully. His thoughts swiftly moved to the sundial locked securely in Mia's suitcase's secret compartment.

"To the airport then," chipped in Granny. "The sooner we leave and solve this mystery, the safer we all are going to be."

"I'll head there now, Nellie," said Pablo as he took a sharp turn to the right. Soon they were driving down a narrow, winding road that followed the coast for miles, past sandy bays and a shimmering turquoise sea. The road then veered to the left which took them through the jungle. As the passengers glanced out the windows they saw the tops of the tall trees joined together like a crowd of vivid green umbrellas over their heads. If it wasn't for the white fluffy cotton-ball clouds that seemed to drift slowly across the sky, they could have sworn dusk was approaching.

Before they knew it, the road turned swiftly to the right and the airport opened up in front of them. Pablo drove the taxi quickly through the private airstrip and parked next to his plane.

"The plane has been refilled with gas and is ready to go. I can take you to Italy, but I can't stay. Spencer and I will need to come back here."

"Understood, Pablo," said Granny. "We appreciate any help you can give us." Pablo nodded and stepped out of the taxi.

"So we're all going?" asked Spencer.

"You'll have to," interjected Morris. "The Panther has left the park. We can't take any chances that he find you. As of right now, I don't believe he knows where we've gone."

"Good, so now let's go," urged Granny as she began to push everyone out of the taxi. She followed behind keeping everyone on track until they reached the stairs to the plane, then she literally pushed everyone up them. Once inside, Granny glanced swiftly at the taxi and their surroundings, before heading inside herself, closing the hatch behind her. The inside of the plane was cool compared to the stifling heat outside. Her body was drenched with sweat. As she glanced at her fellow companions, their clothing also stuck to their bodies, and beads of sweat on their brows and cheeks made them look shiny and slick.

"Everyone, find a seat and buckle up," yelled Pablo as he and Spencer entered the cockpit of the plane. Mia buckled her seatbelt. She glanced around. Max seemed relaxed. Granny was on edge, her keen eyes looking around constantly, while Emmanuel appeared calm, almost defeated. It looked like he felt he had failed in his job to protect the tablets, and yet he had to know that he had done all he

could. Because of their family connection, Mia knew
Emmanuel was still resolved to protect the tablets from the
Panther, but now he had friends to help him. That knowledge should make him feel slightly better. But what would
his grandfather say? Mia thought Emmanuel didn't look
like he was in any hurry to find out.

"We're set up here," called Pablo from the cockpit. "Ready?" He didn't look behind him to see his passengers mixed responses.

It didn't take long to feel the plane moving swiftly down the landing strip and rise from the ground. The
passengers felt pressed against their seats as the plane lifted into the air, the force causing their stomachs to lift
into their throats. When the plane reached its desired
height, it balanced out, and the pressure returned to normal, though all of their ears popped.

As Max glanced out the window, he could see the
ocean. It looked peaceful and calm. Though Max hoped
the weather would remain as beautiful as it was now, he
knew that once they were out into the ocean, the weather could change in an instant. He prayed it would remain
calm. Trying to relax, Max closed his eyes. He wasn't sure
how long it would take them to reach Italy, or what
might lie ahead, so he decided it would be best to save
his energy and rest. He wasn't the only one on his team
to do so. He opened his eyes briefly to glance at Granny
and Mia. They both had their seats lowered slightly and
their eyes were closed. Max turned his head and adjusted his position in his seat. Soon he was fast asleep.

# EIGHTEEN

HOURS PASSED BY THE TIME Max woke up. As his eyes adjusted to the interior of the plane, he noticed that a soft light filled the cabin, allowing him to see. He glanced outside only to observe that the sky was as dark as pitch, and yet clear. As his gaze drifted to his companions, he noticed their sleeping forms. He was not sure what woke him. Could it have been instinct? Max stretched as he glanced out the window again. As his gaze devoured the night, he noticed that the sky was not as clear as he thought. He instantly searched for the moon, which glowed from behind some high clouds and bathed the sky in ghostly reflections. For some reason, Max's heart leapt in his chest. What put him on edge? Max raised his arm and whispered urgently, "Morris!"

"What's up, Max?" Morris' voice was devoid of sleep, which meant that he was determined to stay awake until his team made it to their destination.

"I feel," answered Max. "I feel . . . as if something—"

"Isn't quite right?" added Morris.

"Exactly! How is everything looking?"

"Good so far. The Panther is still in the Riviera Maya, which I have to say is making me feel better. But, for some reason, I am—"

"Waiting for the other shoe to drop?"

Morris knew Max and he were in the same frame of mind. They both were concerned that their escape had come too easily.

"It's scary when you and I think alike," stated Morris.

"You aren't kidding. But if we are thinking alike, that's also a good thing. We're anticipating the worst."

"Let's go through what we know, so we can reason it all out to make sense and see what we have missed," insisted Morris.

"Okay! First, let's go through the players. Walter is CIA. He was helping us and yet not."

"He was certainly on his own agenda," interjected Morris.

"Correct! Then we have the fat man and Marissa Sanchez—both accomplices used by the Panther to do his dirty work. Then, of course our nemesis, the Panther, calling the shots from afar. He was faxing information to the fat man who was then corresponding with Marissa and Walter, who he thought was on his side, and then faxing information back to him. He was clever moving to different places so his fax number couldn't be traced to the same location."

"Now, the items," instructed Morris.

"Yes, the items. We found the *Yupana*, which we believe was stolen by the Panther and put for Granny to find by one of his accomplices. The *Yupana* was supposed to lead us to Machu Picchu in Peru to get us out of the way. Then we have Emmanuel's sundial, and we found one of the tablets—the tablet of the Jaguar— both are important pieces to this puzzle. We also have the Mayan numbers eight and thirteen. I'm not sure what relevance these numbers have yet, but . . ."

"Actually, Max, I think I know. Spencer mentioned some pretty interesting information about the *Yupana*. He said it was an Incan calculator. Researchers assumed that the calculations were based on Fibonacci numbers."

"Eight and thirteen are Fibonacci numbers," added Max.

"Correct!" encouraged Morris. Suddenly, Max's eyes lit up with a revelation.

"Morris, where was Fibonacci from?"

"I'm glad you asked, mate. He was from Italy, around Pisa, I think."

"And where does Emmanuel's grandfather live?"

"In Pisa! Oh, Max, I think I know where you're going with this."

"Good, because I was trying to paint you a vivid picture with a wide brush. I think there's a connection between Dante and this whole mess. He knows way more than what any of us, including Emmanuel, knows. I believe when we get to Italy, he needs to be the first one we see, if he is willing to talk to us or not."

150

"He'll talk to us now, Max. We have the things he cherishes the most," commented Morris wisely. Max glanced over at Emmanuel's sleeping form, then turned his head and drifted off in thought. After some time, he asked Morris, "How are we doing?"

"Good! I'll keep you posted if anything changes. You're currently over halfway to your destination. You should be seeing land, so hang in there. Keep in mind the time change. You are now five to six hours ahead of what you were before."

"Will do. Thank you, mate," and with that, Max lowered his arm and returned his attention to the inside of the plane. Still, something in his gut told him that there was more. Then he heard it—a beeping sound. Max angled his head toward the right. It was coming from somewhere close. His gaze swept the bodies of his sleeping companions, trying to pinpoint the sound. Max slowly unbuckled his seat belt and stood up. He was partially hunched over as he moved closer to the sound. *BEEP! BEEP!* With every step he felt the sound was mocking him. *BEEP! BEEP!*

Determined to find it, Max dropped to his knees. *BEEP! BEEP!* Finally Max came upon the source. Something in Emmanuel's shirt pocket was beeping. Carefully, Max reached into the pocket. His fingertips soon grasped a piece of paper. Gently, Max withdrew it. The piece of paper was folded several times. Max began to unfold the paper. When he did something fell into his hand. It was a tracking device, a miniature, round circle with a red light in the center of it. Someone must have activated it, which was why it just started beeping. No wonder why the Panther was not following closely behind. He didn't have to. He was waiting to see where they were going. Marissa Sanchez must have planted the device when she had confronted Emmanuel.

Max immediately jumped up and went to his backpack on the floor by his seat. He placed the paper in his back pocket before he unzipped the bag and took out a bottle of water. There was only a third of it left, but it'd be enough. Max removed the cap and dropped the device into the water. Within seconds, the red light on the device stopped flashing. Pleased with himself, Max sat back in his seat and recapped his bottle. After staring at it for some time, he decided to throw it away. He stood and walked between the six seats to the back, tossing it nonchalantly in the waste basket that was set into the wall. After he did that, he returned to his seat.

But Max wasn't phased with what he had just done. He sat back calmly, wondering what the Panther might be doing. Then he remembered the piece of paper the tracking device had been wrapped in. He quickly took it from his pocket and unfolded it. There was one word on it, a word that completely eliminated his satisfaction and put fear in his heart.

*BOOM!*

Max only then realized what he had done, and it was too late. Before he could say a word an explosion rocked the plane from the rear. It woke everyone.

Granny screamed while Mia covered her ears, her eyes darting around in panic. Emmanuel sheltered his head from the debris while glancing out the window. He saw black smoke with reddish-yellow flames coming from the engines. The plane started losing altitude. Max knew Pablo was yelling at them in warning as the plane began to go down. All Max could hear was Morris's voice as he yelled through his watch, "Don't worry, I'll find you! Just stay alive! Whatever you do, don't give up. I'll find you! I *will* find you!"

## THE END

To be continued in Book Four.

## ETH THECS FO YMRYETS